TIME OF MY LIFE

LAURA HEFFERNAN

SHE'S A POOR DANCE TEACHER. HE'S HER RICH STUDENT. IF THEY CAN ONLY OVERCOME THEIR DIFFERENCES, THIS COULD BE LOVE

Janey's never felt this way before, but staff is forbidden from dating passengers. It's only one dirty dance, what could go wrong?

Legend says everyone who boards the Oceanic Aphrodite finds love. Janey's on the ship to teach pole fitness, not for romance. Then she meets Frank. He's everything Janey isn't–refined, classy, rich–but his good looks and charm make him undeniably appealing. Unfortunately, he's also a passenger.

When Janey's partner can't perform in the end-of-cruise talent show, Frank offers to fill in. He's never done pole, but she's got time to teach him. As they grow closer, Janey finds herself hoping the legend is real–but if she gives in to temptation, she could be out of a job.

COPYRIGHT

To Heather T.

Thank you for helping me find my inner diva.

CHAPTER ONE

DAY ONE: MIAMI

Right, left, up, swing left leg around, climb, fall backward, pause. The steps for my doubles routine went through my head on repeat while I stood in line at security, waiting to go through the inspection point and board the Oceanic *Aphrodite.* For the first time, I'd be dancing the Talent Show finale at the end of the cruise, which needed to go flawlessly. My future depended on this event, so I practiced every possible second.

My toes tapped in time with my thoughts, probably making me look quite odd. Fortunately, I'd been sailing this cruise for months as part of the onboard entertainment. The officers working the line knew me, and they were used to watching me dance in line. Once I made it to the metal detectors, it should be smooth sailing. Pun intended.

Normally, staff boarded the ship the night before or early in the morning before any guests arrived. My cabin mate Penny and I had gotten special permission to spend the night off-ship, a privilege that likely wouldn't be repeated now that her guy problems made us two hours late. At least they'd agreed to let us on right after the VIPs so we could beat most of the regular passengers.

Beside me, Penny tapped away on her phone, her long dark hair forming a curtain over the device. "Why hasn't Robbie texted me back?"

"I'm sure you'll hear from him soon." I struggled to keep from revealing my true feelings on the subject. "Especially since he'll be on the ship. It's not like he can avoid you forever."

Her head shot up, brown eyes flashing. "You think he's avoiding me?"

In truth, yes, I did. But if I hadn't been distracted thinking about our upcoming performance, I would have found a nicer way to say so. Well, probably. I'd been trying to politely tell her what a creep Robbie was for weeks, and she hadn't listened. Maybe it was time to be more direct. "I think he enjoys the rich passengers who might further his career once he graduates. Rob's pretty clear on his priorities, and you're not one of them."

"Ouch." Her face twisted into a grimace. A pang hit me. "I hope you're wrong."

"So do I, Pen. So do I." Not knowing what else to say, I changed the subject. "I'm excited that Max is letting us do the finale this week."

"Oh, I know! It's going to be amazing! The guests won't know what hit 'em. Especially the stuffy old farts who think pole dancing is only for strippers."

Despite myself, I blanched.

A look of horror crossed her face. "Oh, no. I'm sorry, Janey."

She hadn't meant to insult me, but I'd learned pole while working strip clubs. The patrons loved blue-eyed blondes, so owners always wanted someone with my look.

"It's fine," I said, breaking the awkward silence.

If things went well this week, the two of us would be cemented as dancing partners for the next year of cruises or more. Each additional performance meant cash in our pockets. I could ignore one thoughtless comment in the interests of continuing to pay for my father's assisted living every month. Dad had nowhere else to go, especially since his disability left him unable to care for himself.

Needing to look at anything else, I turned to face the metal detectors separating us from the ship's boarding area. The line of people might as well be a wall. I shifted from one six-inch heel to the other, wondering what this week's hold-up was. Last week, a bride didn't understand why her father couldn't bring his actual guns to her "shotgun" wedding. The week before, a groom tried to bring a case of whiskey, which is against ship policy. Maybe we had a celebrity up ahead. They always slowed down security. Rumor had it that some famous baseball player was getting married onboard this week. I didn't follow sports, though, so unless he wore his uniform, I'd never know.

Craning my neck to see the inevitable shenanigans at the front of the line, I almost didn't hear the commotion behind me. A woman gasped, then a child cried out. I turned to see what was happening, a fraction of a second too late.

A man's voice yelled, "Look out!"

Seconds later, something shoved me from behind, hard. Stumbling, I wheeled my arms for balance. The heel cracked off my shoe. I tumbled to the ground, landing hard on my hip. Ouch. As a dancer, I'm no stranger to injuries, but that was going to leave a bruise. It stung, almost as much as the realization that I was going to have to replace my two hundred dollar Pleasers—and with no time to go shopping before we set sail, I'd have to do it at one of the ship's outrageously overpriced boutiques. Entertainment staff got a discount, but not nearly enough. Silently, I kissed this week's earnings good-bye. At least I didn't have to pay for my room, utilities, or food.

"Are you okay?" The same voice asked.

Blinking several times to clear the pain clouding my vision, I looked up to see such a delicious-looking man bending over me, I wondered if I imagined him. Curly brown hair falling across his forehead, light brown eyes the color of a latte, high cheekbones, a strong nose, and perfect lips. This face belonged in a museum.

"Gorgeous," I said without thinking. Then I flushed. "I mean, yes. I'm okay. What happened?"

His lips twitched at my slip of the tongue. "Runaway baggage cart. You were nearly murdered by a wedding dress. What an unfortunate end for such a talented fidgeter."

"You saw me dancing?"

"I may have noticed you before the cart rolled away."

The admission made me smile. "Well, thanks. If you hadn't been here, I might have been flattened."

"Glad I could help." He held out a hand to pull me to my feet. Our eyes locked, and suddenly, I couldn't breathe. "I'm Frank."

"Janey. Nice to meet you." As perfected over the years, I kept my face and tone pleasant but not overly friendly. As hot as this guy was, passengers were strictly forbidden. I didn't want to spend the entire cruise wishing he wasn't. Dropping his hand, I moved away from him, back toward the line.

A wince of pain sent me looking for the nearest chair. The fall must've twisted my ankle, and I'd been too distracted by this man to notice. Frank had shifted away, following my lead, but now he returned to my side. "Are you okay?"

"It's nothing. I'll walk it off."

"Let me see."

"It's no big deal," I insisted. "I'm a dancer. Happens far more often than it should."

"That's unfortunate, but please let me see it. It's my fault you're hurt, and I'm a doctor."

"Don't worry about me. Penny, are you okay?"

My friend stood nearby, her face unreadable. "It missed me by a mile. But I'm a little dizzy. I've got to go. I'll see you onboard."

Before I could tell her not to go call deadbeat Robbie again, she vanished in the direction of the women's restroom, one hand resting on her stomach. Poor thing. My friend needed me, and I wanted to go with her, but my throbbing ankle stopped me. I didn't want to spent more time falling under Dr. Frank's spell, but the line to get onto the ship–and to the infirmary–hadn't budged. Better to sit and let him check me out than stand in pain, balancing on a broken shoe.

Together, we hobbled to a bench near the entrance to the security line. It wasn't nearly as far away as it should have been after twenty minutes of waiting. I collapsed with a sigh. Then my eyes landed on something and I groaned. "Oh, no."

"What's wrong?" Frank asked.

"My carry-on is still in the line. I need to grab it before someone reports it to security as an unattended bag."

"Is it that green one?" He pointed at my battered duffel, now sitting a bit outside the line, probably pushed by an overeager passenger. "That's all you need for a week?"

The bag only contained a few things I'd taken to spend the night at my sister's apartment, playing dress-up with my five-year-old niece. Easily the best thing about having a home port in Miami. Everything else remained in the cabin Penny and I shared. This passenger didn't need to know that.

"Yeah."

"Don't move." He touched my shoulder as he walked away, sending an unexpected jolt of desire through me. Oh, no. The last thing I needed was to get involved with a passenger, and this one could be trouble.

As my savior walked away, I marveled at his straight back,

the way he held his head erect. The man moved with confidence, but also an innate grace, like a cat. Or a dancer. He didn't walk, he glided across the floor. I also took in the lines of his windbreaker, the creases of his pants, the leather of the shoes molding to his feet perfectly. Dr. Frank was off-limits for more reasons than one. Rich men only ever wanted one thing from girls like me, and I wasn't in a position to give it.

A moment later, he returned, my bag slung over his shoulder. I thanked him, then lifted my injured leg to rest on top once he set it in front of me. The pain subsided, so I scooted down to rest my head on top of the bench. Perfect. Except for being late to work and the throbbing ankle.

"I'm going to check you out now, okay?"

It was on the tip of my tongue to mention that I'd been checking him out for the last five minutes, but flirting with passengers needed to remain subtler, more innocent. I nodded. His touch was firm, yet soft. He poked and prodded for a moment while I did my best not to wince.

Finally, he said, "It's not broken."

Relief washed over me. If I broke my ankle, I'd be out of a job. While I loved my sister and niece, I didn't want to move in with them after becoming unemployed and homeless. "Thank goodness."

"Wrap it up for a couple of days, try to stay off it, and you should be fine. The infirmary will have elastic bandages."

"I've got one in my bag, actually," I said, opening a zipper on the side. "Part of the job."

"Excellent! Please, allow me."

I should say no, do it myself. After all, I'd wrapped various body parts a thousand times. But the smallest innocent touch couldn't hurt anything. His firm hands warmed my ankle, making it feel better already. Once we got on the ship, I'd never see him again. "Thanks."

He took the bandage and expertly wrapped my ankle in a matter of seconds. His hand lingered, just enough for me to notice. This magnetic pull between us wasn't one-sided. "There you go."

For the first time, I noticed how close he stood. The heat of his breath washed over my cheek. My skin burned where he'd examined my ankle. I refused to let myself wonder what these fingers would feel like moving over the rest of my body. He licked his lips, and my eyes darted involuntarily to follow the movement. I became helpless to look away.

It had been a long time since I'd been with anyone. Too long. I made a mental note to find a suitable hookup at the first port. Suitable meaning not a passenger, and not while on the ship. Not if I wanted to keep my job, which I very much enjoyed.

"Are you part of the Sassy Singles?" I asked, naming a group that booked multiple activities for passengers interested in meeting someone.

"Me? No, I'm not looking for a relationship." Good. Neither was I. Not that it mattered. He continued. "But it cracks me up that they'd put a singles cruise on a ship called the *Aphrodite*."

"Well, legend has it that people fall in love on this ship. One day, and you'll meet your mate. Or so they say."

"Huh. Good thing I believe in science over myth then."

"Yeah," I said, shaking off an inexplicable twinge of disappointment. The legend was a marketing ploy; all the staff knew it. After all, we'd been sailing around for months without falling in love. But it sold tickets for the singles cruises.

"Francis!" A high-pitched voice broke the spell between us.

Over the doctor's shoulder I spotted a stunningly gorgeous woman in flawless heavy makeup, chestnut hair with the top half twisted elegantly into a sleek chignon, and a swingy white sundress with big pink flowers painted all over it.

"Over here," he called to the woman.

"Francis, huh?"

"It's a family name."

"I'm sure it is." The longer we talked, the more dangerously close I came to crossing a line, but I couldn't resist one more comment before reining it in. "After the first woman in the cabinet?"

He grinned. "How'd you guess?"

The question was a joke, so his response startled me. I blinked a couple of times to cover my surprise before responding. "My mother was a big *Dirty Dancing* fan. I've got that and *Lethal Weapon* memorized."

What I didn't mention was that those were the only two videos we'd owned. After Mom walked out on me and my sister, those movies were my only way of feeling connected to her. I wore out the DVDs, watching them over and over.

"A woman of refined tastes," he said.

Before I could respond, the woman arrived at Frank's side, placing a perfectly manicured hand on his shoulder. She said nothing, her expression stormy, eyes hidden behind sunglasses the size of Disney World.

"Hey, Lisa," he said. "Is it time?"

"'Is it time?'" she mimicked, her face twisting into a grimace. "Duh! We're going to be late! Get your butt in line."

Girlfriend? Wife? No. No rings on either of them. My heart sank. Of course a man like Frank would have a girlfriend. Charming, sexy, rich, a doctor who moved with the grace of a dancer? The fact that I'd spent even half a second thinking he might be available made me flush with embarrassment. Especially when he'd said he wasn't looking for a relationship–he wouldn't be if he were here with someone.

On the other hand, this *was* a singles cruise, so maybe there was hope. The two of them had similar coloring, the same nose.

As I took in the shapes of their faces, I'd bet my favorite Pleasers that she was related to Frank.

With a sigh, I glanced at my feet. Second favorite pair, anyway. These were toast.

"We can't be late. The ship isn't going to disembark with VIP passengers waiting to go through the security line," he said, but he stood to follow her.

Of course he was a VIP. The sunglasses pushed casually on top of his head cost more than half my Pleasers collection. The shoes I needed for work and had been accumulating slowly over the past ten years, most of them from eBay. We didn't move in the same circles. I couldn't even afford to window shop in his world.

"What if it does, though? Won't you feel terrible?" She spoke slowly, as if addressing an unintelligent child. She must be an older sister; younger siblings never got away with talking like that. I had to believe Frank wouldn't date someone who treated him like something stuck to the bottom of her shoe. "I can't believe this. I should be sipping champagne right now."

I craned my neck up to meet her eyes from my seated position. "The VIP passengers are the first to board. You'll have over an hour to relax and explore the ship while the non-VIPs are going through security downstairs. Unless you turn around and leave the port area, you'll be fine."

"Thanks," the woman said icily. She gave me a practiced once over before turning back to Frank. "Who is this and why are you talking to her instead of going through security?"

"I'm Janey. I work–"

She put her hand out in the 'stop' sign. "That's nice. We have to go."

"So, uh, that's my sister," Frank said as Lisa stalked away. Unlike her brother, she moved like a linebacker.

"Seems delightful."

"Being late stresses her out. She's usually not so bad. Anyway, looks like we made it to the front of the line." A couple watched us from the space directly in front of the metal detectors as Lisa walked through. Frank gestured at them. "Those are my friends, Jake and Margie. Do you want to join us so you don't have to wait?"

From the other side of security, Lisa turned, hands on hips. "Francis Hanson, now!"

If the rest of his party was anything like her, the last thing I wanted was to hang out with them. "Thanks, but I'll wait for Penny. I don't want to get on your sister's bad side."

"You're right about that." He laughed. "I've got to go. Sorry."

"It's cool. Thanks again for saving me." Before I finished my sentence, he'd jogged off to meet his party.

Watching him go, I sighed. Well, it was a nice moment, before Lisa showed up. Probably for the best, given our circumstances.

I pulled myself upright, testing my sore ankle. Not terrible, not great. I was supposed to dance in this evening's welcome show, though, and that might not be possible.

Digging around in my bag, I found a pair of flip flops in the bottom. Switching shoes helped. Then I went to find Penny. She hadn't gone far, standing outside the bathroom near the row of pay phones. In all my months working for the cruise line, this was the first time I'd seen anyone looking like they might use one.

I didn't ask if she'd managed to get through to Robbie, preferring to believe she hadn't tried. I was afraid she used a pay phone to try to trick him into answering her call, which made me sad. Penny deserved so much better. At least she put her phone away and returned to the line with me.

The rest of the VIPs had finished going through security and waited for the gangway to open. Through the crowd, I spotted the captain's hat bobbing toward the giant glass doors. A glance at the clock on the wall told me he would be boarding soon, and this area would clear out quickly.

Scooping up my bag, I went through the line in record time. The throbbing in my ankle had dulled to an ache, and I thought about finding Dr. Frank to thank him again. Probably a bad idea, given the chemistry between us, but also the polite thing to do.

Then I spotted him, through the glass separating the waiting area from the docks. He walked about five steps behind the Captain. Beside him strode Lisa, the couple from the security line, and two people I recognized with a start. Only very special guests got priority boarding, which reinforced that this guy was way out of my league. But what sealed our lack of fate was the person who walked beside Frank's friend: my boss, Max Weiss.

Consorting with the passengers was strictly prohibited. If I did anything beyond extremely innocent flirtation with Frank, and Max found out about it, I would get fired and left at the nearest port.

Ahead of Max walked the ship owner's very beautiful, very single daughter, Nellie. In response to something Frank said, she threw her head back, letting out a laugh I knew from experience was throaty and very sexy. Where Nellie went, heads turned. I couldn't begin to compete with her, even if doing so wouldn't cost me my job. As I watched, she reached out and touched Frank on the shoulder. He slung one arm around her casually in an intimate gesture. My heart sank.

Time for this particular fantasy to sail off into the horizon.

CHAPTER TWO

The first night of the cruise, the staff provided multiple forms of onboard entertainment. Dancers like me mostly either did a Rockettes-type routine in the theater or assisted one of the Assistant Cruise Directors in the Welcome Show, held on the main stage in the auditorium. A few of the newer girls helped with a dating game-style show or collected answers at trivia. I'd worked all of those jobs at one time or another. Getting chosen for the Welcome Show was a big honor, even though the job itself entailed little more than smiling pretty and giving fake laughs at terrible jokes. Still, it was an extremely visible position. Visibility could lead to more head-lining gigs and more bonuses. Better yet, it could lead to offers from competing cruise lines.

This season, Penny earned the lead spot in the show. She'd picked me to assist, and the two of us had gotten into a groove over the last couple of months. I had even less responsibility than she did, mostly walking around the audience and handing people a microphone when they needed to say something. Mindless work, but way better than watching the awkwardness of the dating show. My ankle throbbed a bit by the end of the night, but it would be fine once I got more ice and a good night's sleep.

After the show, I removed my makeup, changed, and gathered with the other entertainers in the staff room. Not just the few staff members from the Welcome Aboard show, but the dancers who opened the headline act in the theater, and the groups that sang in the casino, bars, and various nightclubs scattered throughout the ship. Virtually everyone had to work early in the morning, so the gathering wouldn't go late, but we needed to blow off steam after a long day. Somewhere away from the passengers and more senior cruise staff.

The "upper echelon staff" were all smiles and friendly banter in the public areas, but most of them considered the dancers little better than vermin. Classism was alive and well in the cruise industry. As an American, I got slightly better treatment than the members of the wait staff, but all of us were beneath the highest tier employees: the men who ran things, mostly white, all from English-speaking countries.

Whatever. We did our work, we got paid. Period. As much as I wanted to care how other employees were treated, life long ago taught me to look out for myself first. Hierarchy of needs and all that.

While my mind wandered, my gaze did the same, searching the room for Penny. She vanished after the show, which made me worry that she still felt sick. After my third scan of the room, I decided to go find her.

Three steps later, I stopped as a mountain stepped into my path. More accurately, a wall of man with dark, wavy hair and a shiny black t-shirt plastered to his myriad muscles. Androtimos, who tended bar at the Kosmos Lounge and seemed to be in competition with Robbie to see who could delude more women into sleeping with him.

"Leaving so soon, my butterfly?" The term of endearment

made my lips twitch with amusement. He called all the women that.

Ignoring his question, I said, "Have you seen Penny?"

"Sorry, no. I'm on break. But if you want, I'll keep an eye out for her. Why don't you come by my cabin when I get off?"

"Thanks, but no." I started to walk around him.

"Janey, wait." He put one hand on my arm. "Let's talk about this."

The last thing I wanted was to talk more to this guy who couldn't take no for an answer. I cast a glance around the room, hoping desperately I'd spot Penny and have an excuse to walk away. I didn't see her, but I did notice someone else I recognized. Even at this distance, the cut of his clothes and shine of his shoes labelled him an outsider. If I got closer, the fabric would be deliciously soft beneath my fingertips, the designer label one I'd never dream of purchasing.

"Sorry, but I have to go talk to someone." I nodded toward Frank, not sounding sorry in the least. Quickly, I stepped around Androtimos before he could reply and approached our interloper. "Hey! What are you doing here?"

"I carried a watermelon."

The words didn't make any sense, especially his hands held nothing. A loud din filled the room, though, so I leaned forward and asked him to repeat himself.

Frank's breath warmed my ear, sending a shiver down my spine. "I said 'I carried a watermelon.' You're not the only one who can quote *Dirty Dancing*."

I chuckled. "Thought you weren't a fan."

"I'm not. After our earlier conversation, I googled famous lines." He flushed slightly, then looked away. Those dimples and that "Aww, shucks" look must be popular with the ladies back home. "It was 'I carried a watermelon' or 'nobody puts Baby in the corner,' but that wouldn't have answered your question."

A warm, fuzzy feeling buzzed in my chest. You could drive a truck through the smile spreading across my face, despite issuing myself yet another warning that Frank was off limits. "I made one movie reference, and you googled famous lines?"

"There's not a lot to do around here," he deadpanned. "Okay, okay...I was practicing what to say next time I saw you."

"You do that often? Practice talking to women?"

"Almost never," he said. "But I couldn't stop thinking about you. Is your ankle okay?"

"Oh." Right. Those sparks were all in my head. He was just being a conscientious doctor. "Yeah, good as new. Thanks."

"I'm glad to hear it," he said.

"Thanks for checking in." I stood and faked a huge yawn. "It's been a long day. I better get back to my cabin."

"Can I walk with you? I'd like to check on your friend."

His request put me on edge. This funny, charming guy was also super rich and rubbing elbows with the big boss. I couldn't have him spying on me and gossiping with his friends.

"Why?" The question came out sharper than intended, but I needed to know what he knew or suspected.

"She said she felt dizzy down on the docks. During the show, a couple of times, she seemed shaky."

Oh, no. This was so bad. "You haven't said anything to anyone else, have you?"

"No. Should I? I figured the luggage cart got to her."

I grasped the excuse like a life raft. "Yeah, it really freaked her out. Does Max know you're down here?"

He shook his head, expression unreadable. "Max? The cruise guy?"

"I saw you talking to him earlier. You seemed pretty chatty."

He grimaced. "What a dick. He and my friend Jake were frat brothers. Jake thought sucking up to him might get us a free meal at one of the five star restaurants. I've never seen Max before and doubt I'll talk to him again."

"Good to know," I said. "He wouldn't approve of his friends hanging out with the entertainment staff."

"My lips are sealed," he said. "I guess I should be going."

"Yes, you should," I said. "I'll see you around. I was on my way out, too."

"Does that mean we can walk together?"

He seemed sincere. It was on the tip of my tongue to say yes. I liked talking to Frank, and my eyes devoured every inch of him. Unfortunately, I couldn't afford the risk. "I'm sorry, but dancers aren't allowed to hang out with passengers when we're not working."

"Some rules were made to be broken. Come on, live a little."

"Maybe in your world," I said, resisting the urge to roll my eyes. "I can't afford to break the rules."

The smile fell off his face. "That's not fair. You don't even know me."

"You're right. I'm not allowed to know you. If you want to book a lesson, I'll see you in the dance studio."

"Great! What do you teach?"

"Pole."

A confused look crossed his face. This was usually when I stopped to explain pole fitness, how it differed from exotic dancing, and how empowering the classes could be. But I didn't have it in me. I needed to get away from this guy.

He opened his mouth to respond, but I swept by him and headed for the door. With a superhuman effort, I avoided turning around to see if Frank watched me go. I spent my days teaching women confidence, and if there was one thing I knew, it was how to pretend I didn't care.

CHAPTER THREE

*P*enny wasn't in our cabin. She also wasn't in the studio, the attached locker room, or the laundry room. Out of desperation, I checked every restaurant on the Lido deck in case she'd had a late night craving, but no dice. I did spot Robbie talking to a group of passengers, so at least they weren't together. Unfortunately, I couldn't interrupt to ask if he knew where she was.

Cell phones didn't work at sea, so I didn't have a contract. My prepaid card ran out back in Florida. After about twenty minutes of searching, panic started to rise in my chest. Standing at the railing, I forced myself to draw several deep breaths. She couldn't have gone far. There was no way off the ship once we left the port. Yet it was a big ship, with many places to hide.

Finally, I headed back to our room, thinking if nothing else, I could use the phone there to call some of the other dancers. Maybe someone had seen her.

As I stepped off the elevator, someone called my name. I stopped, peering through the dimly lit room to see who approached. Guillermo, a member of the cleaning staff. Not running down the hall, but not moving at a leisurely pace.

My jaw dropped when I realized Frank followed directly behind him. "What's going on?" I asked in Spanish.

To my surprise, Frank spoke first, also in Spanish. "You need to come with us."

Guillermo answered my question while Frank started down the stairs. "It's Penelope."

At that, I abandoned my questions and ran to keep up. When we stopped at the elevator, I nodded toward Frank. To Guillermo, I said, "What's he doing here?"

"I found her," Frank said. "And you're welcome. I could have left her, you know."

"*Lo siento*," I said. He was right, of course. My concern for my friend consumed me, overtaking basic human politeness. At the same time, I didn't want to waste time explaining things to a passenger if Penny was in so much trouble they needed to find me. "Guillermo can take me from here. We don't want to take away from your plans for the rest of the evening."

"I don't know where she is," Guillermo said. "This man just asked me to bring him to you."

"Thanks again," Frank said to him.

The elevator doors dinged open, and Frank took off down the hall. I followed at his heels with Guillermo close behind me. "Okay, where's Penny?"

"I found her, throwing up into a sink. In the staff kitchen behind the casino."

Passengers walked through the casino to get to the amphitheater where Penny and I performed earlier. It made such perfect sense, I kicked myself for not looking there myself. But Frank didn't have any business in that area. "How did you get in?"

His face turned red. "Nellie was giving me a tour."

Of course she was. As the owner's daughter, the same rules didn't apply to Nellie as the rest of us. She could take passengers into restricted areas. She could flirt with them and promise the world and walk away with shiny gifts, while the rest of us couldn't even accept tips over a certain amount. She could even date paying guests. I swallowed my disappointment. "Did she see Penny?"

"No. Nellie was talking as she opened the door. I saw Penny, told Nellie I was tired from the long day, and walked her back to her room. Then I came to find you."

"Thanks."

Frank led me down one hallway, up another, and through a door requiring my employee ID for access. Finally, we wound up in one of the room service kitchens, empty and unused this time of night. I glanced around before turning back to Frank with a shrug. "Is this some kind of joke?"

Behind me, Guillermo went to a table in the far corner and crouched on the ground. "She's here."

I went to her and fell to my knees. My friend sat beneath the table, legs tucked to her chest, hair matted to her head. Mascara streaked down her face. My heart broke at the sight. "You told him, didn't you?"

She nodded, and I crawled under the table, hugging her to my chest.

"What's wrong?" Frank asked. Until he spoke, I'd forgotten he was still there. "Told who what?"

"Don't worry about it," I said. If he knew, he'd tell Nellie, and we'd all be in trouble. "We appreciate your concern, but I'll take it from here. Go back to your girlfriend."

"Nellie? We've known each other since we were kids," he said.

Even better, childhood sweethearts. He spent his formative years traveling in circles I didn't know existed. "It's none of my business."

Ignoring me, Guillermo said, "She's pregnant."

"Jesus, Gui, what are you doing?" I asked. "Trying to get us fired?"

Penny barked out a humorless laugh, a hollow sound that sent chills down my spine. "It doesn't matter anymore. Let's tell everyone. Stupid lovesick Penny got knocked up by Robbie, who is absolutely the worst."

"Jake's frat brother Robbie?"

"Who's Jake?" Penny asked.

"One of the friends I came on the cruise with. He was in the security line with me."

I shrugged. "Robbie probably is an overgrown frat boy. He's the head waiter here."

"Yeah, I know him." Frank said. Did this guy know everyone? "I'm sure once you tell him–"

"He knows," Penny said dully, confirming my suspicions. "And now you know, and now you'll tell your little girlfriend, and we're all screwed."

"What if I do tell Nellie?" Frank asked. "What does it matter?"

"Oh, no big deal," I said, trying to ignore the way my stomach lurched when he called Nellie his girlfriend. "A pregnant dancer who can't dance is no use to our bosses. She'll get fired. No big deal to a moneybags like you, I'm sure."

"You think you've got me all figured out," he said. "You don't know anything about me."

"Yeah, I'm sure it sucks to be rich and successful and good-looking," I said. "Not to mention having rich, powerful friends. Do you even know what it's like to wonder where your next meal's coming from? Any of us would trade places with you in a heartbeat."

Frank rolled his eyes, but didn't respond.

I turned to Penny. "What are you doing under there?"

"I heard someone at the door, so I hid. Then they left, but I didn't feel well enough to get up."

Poor thing. As if getting dumped wasn't bad enough. While we spoke, I'd backed out from under the table, keeping hold of Penny's hand. Once I got into a clear space, I tugged, drawing her inch by inch with me.

As soon as we cleared the table, I stood and tried to lift Penny. Pole made me strong, but my friend was tall. As a fellow dancer, she weighed as much as I did. Combined with the fact that her state made her dead weight in my arms, I stumbled. Guillermo caught me.

"*Gracias*," I said.

Frank stepped up. "Let me help."

"Thanks, but I've got her."

"No you don't," Guillermo said. "Let him help you. I've got to go before Max finds out I left my post."

My arms shook. I didn't want to accept Frank's help, but at the same time, didn't know how I'd get Penny back to our cabin by myself. "Are you sure you can handle her? Examining patients isn't exactly manual labor."

"I used to dance ballet," he retorted. "I understand hard work, and I'm strong."

Penny whistled under her breath, the first sound she'd uttered since we arrived.

"You're a doctor who dances?" For a millisecond, I gazed at him, wondering why the universe would send me the perfect man who I couldn't have. He started to answer, but I cut him off. "It doesn't matter. We have to get out of here."

"Then let's go."

"Do you mind if Frank carries you?" I asked Penny.

She shook her head and reached out for him. He took her from me, as gentle as if she were made of glass. Begrudgingly, I let go.

"Lead the way," he said.

Carefully, we skulked out of the kitchen. I breathed a tiny sigh of relief once we made it to the deck, but we weren't out of the woods yet. Guests didn't usually carry performers around the ship, so we needed to stay out of sight.

I slowed my pace because the only thing that would seem stranger than the three of us out in the first place is if I ran while Frank chased me down the deck holding Penny. None of us said a word until we were safely inside our cabin.

I flipped on the lights while Frank carried Penny further into the room. He looked at our bunk beds, the lack of a window. Crew cabins barely fit the people required to sleep in them.

"It's...cozy," he said. "Which bed?"

I pointed at the lower bunk. He laid Penny down so gently, it made me think a little better of him. Of course, he was a doctor so it made sense that he'd treat people with care. It wasn't his fault he'd been born rich any more than it was my fault I wasn't.

"Thanks." Penny stood, then swayed, grabbing onto the bedpost for support. "I need to get cleaned up."

"Are you okay?" Frank asked.

"Fine." A full-body heave sold her out. She bolted for the bathroom, one hand over her mouth. The retching sounds carried clearly to our ears.

"Morning sickness?"

I shook my head. "Apparently, it lasts all day."

He made a sympathetic noise. "That happens with some women. Why doesn't she go to the infirmary?"

"Like I said, pregnant dancers can't dance," I said. "Especially ones who spend several hours a day throwing up."

"Ahhh," he said. "She's got hyperemesis gravidarum?"

"Huh?"

"Violent nausea, all the time. Lots of throwing up. Sometimes requires hospitalization. The Duchess of Cambridge had it with all three children."

"Who?"

"Some people call her Princess Kate. William's wife." I stared at him until he said, "Diana and Charles's eldest son? Second in line for the throne of England."

The idea that he thought I had any idea of the Royal Family's medical issues told me volumes about our differences. Ten seconds ago, I couldn't have told you how many kids Kate and William had. I shrugged. "I'm no doctor, but maybe. She's sick all the time. It's awful."

"There's not a lot she can do, but staying hydrated and being monitored by a doctor will do wonders. She might need to take time off until it passes."

The casual way he suggested not working brought my hackles up. "Easy, right? Of course, if she doesn't work, she doesn't get paid, so there's no money. She's not allowed on the ship unless she's working, so she won't have a place to live or money to get one. She can only visit the infirmary while onboard. Oh, and the cruise line doesn't provide health insurance, so good luck paying for a doctor anywhere else."

"What about FMLA? Anti-discrimination laws?"

"Cruise ships aren't American. Most of the companies, including Oceanic, are registered in Panama. U.S. law doesn't apply."

His features softened as I spoke. "I get it. Your friend is in a bad situation."

"Yeah."

"What are you going to do?"

"Well, for now, I'm going to go in there, smooth her hair back, and hold her hand until she feels well enough to go to bed," I said. "I've been covering for her as much as I can. Swapping shifts and making deals with the other performers to get her into things like Bingo or Trivia Night, where she can sit and smile and not have to move much."

"Janey is doing way too much," Penny said from the bathroom doorway. Until she spoke, I hadn't realized she listened to us. "I tried to get pills while we were in Miami, but the doctor said I'd have to pay for them."

"That's great!" Frank said.

"Not great," she said. "It's nine hundred dollars for a three-week supply."

My mouth fell open. I'd known that she'd requested pills, but not the exorbitant cost. No way we could afford something like that, especially not when she might need them for nine months for all we knew.

"I don't suppose you'd accept a loan," Frank said.

"From you? Of course not. I can't pay you back. And it's too late now, anyway. Thanks for your help tonight."

"You're welcome," he said. "Do you need anything else?"

"Not unless you know a way I can dance in the Talent Show on Friday," Penny said. "I'd hoped everything would work out, but without those pills, there's no way I'll make it. Janey and I will both lose our bonus if we don't perform. It's a doubles routine. She can't do it alone."

"Penny!" The last thing we needed was Nellie's little boyfriend even *more* in our business.

"A doubles routine, huh?" Frank asked.

"Yeah. We're demonstrating pole moves. If it goes well, they'll book us to do the same routine on other cruises, and the bonuses are awesome. But I've been too sick to practice," Penny said. "The rocking of the ship makes it worse."

"She can't do the routine alone?" Frank asked.

"I could," I said, "but then it's not a doubles routine. It's not nearly as impressive as what Max wants. That means no bonus. They'll find someone else to close out the Talent Show going forward. And I can't afford to lose the money." He didn't need to know how Dad depended on me. My sister had no extra money to help, not as a single mom.

"Can't somebody else fill in?"

"Who?" I gestured around the room in a wide, sweeping motion. As wide as one could get in a space the size of a closet occupied by three people, at least. "You've got a surplus of pole dancers hiding on the ship? It's not exactly as common as ballet."

His face flushed. "I realize that, but you've got a huge team of entertainers here."

"Show dancers. Broadway-types. If I needed someone to do tap or hip-hop, most of them could dive into the show in a heartbeat. But I've just started teaching pole this season, and the entertainers don't get time off work to attend classes. We've all got our own stuff," I said. "One of the other dancers is strong, and she could probably do the moves, but she doesn't have time to learn the routine."

"Not to mention," Penny said, "that most of them would jump at the opportunity to steal the finale and make it their own. They'd want the bonus for themselves, both this week and every cruise from now on."

"You're not going to be able to dance much over the next few months, anyway," Frank said.

"If we can find a way to do Friday night's show, we'll figure something out," Penny said. "We're off for two weeks before we report to the Alaska cruise at the beginning of May. Morning sickness is only supposed to last the first trimester, right? I'm getting close."

"Give it up, Pen," I said hollowly. The more we talked about this, the bigger the pit in my stomach grew. "It's not going to happen."

Frank said, "Come on, there's got to be someone–"

"What? You want to do it?" I laughed hollowly. As if.

He shook his head. "I don't know the first thing about pole."

"Now there's an idea," Penny said.

"It's an idea, alright. A *terrible* one." I couldn't believe my friend thought I should spend *more* time with Nellie's boyfriend.

"He's got the right build." She walked around Frank, eyeing him up and down like a prized racehorse. At least she didn't lift his lips to check out his gums and teeth. "And he's got the background. You said you used to dance?"

"Ballet, yeah."

"It's not that different," she said.

My lips twitched with amusement. Not that different? "Go on."

"Both require a lot of strength. Flexibility. Grace. You've seen it yourself. When someone comes to a class with a ballet or dance background, they pick pole up no problem."

"That's true," I admitted begrudgingly. "They still need more than a week to pick up the more advanced moves."

"So we make a few changes, take out the super difficult stuff. You're a wonderful teacher, Janey. You can teach anyone."

I turned to Frank. "This is one problem you can't throw money at. You said you wanted to help. Is that true?"

"Yeah, I want to help. And I do miss performing. You think I can do it?"

"Let's find out," I said.

"Take off your shoes," Penny told him. "You're about to get a crash course."

They both looked at me. Part of me wanted to walk away. But Frank had the right background. I'd already noted how gracefully he moved. More importantly, he was our only option. If we didn't do the performance, we'd lose money I sorely needed. Max would dump us ashore in a heartbeat.

I could manage. After all, I'd always been poor. I could get by, skip a few meals, sleep in some parks until I found a new job. Not the end of the world. But Penny had grown up comfortably, the daughter of two Cuban refugees who ran a very successful restaurant. Upper middle class, which was rich to me. She didn't know what it was like to go to bed hungry or to walk around in the dark all winter because you couldn't afford lights. Her parents cut her off when she told them she wanted to be a dancer instead of taking over the family business.

Even if I could screw Penny over, I certainly couldn't do that to her unborn child. The baby deserved better. He or she might grow up without a father thanks to Robbie's unwillingness to help, but Aunt Janey would fight tooth and nail to get that baby whatever he or she needed.

One look at Penny sealed my fate. She worried her lower lip between her teeth, eyebrows drawn together. I knew all the same thoughts swirled around in both our heads. The only difference was, I had the power to give her peace of mind.

I turned to Frank and held out my hand. "Let's do this."

CHAPTER FOUR

DAY TWO: AT SEA

On the first full day of the cruise, I taught back-to-back pole classes starting early in the morning. Finding it a bit awkward to walk down the deck wearing five-inch heels, a feather boa, a tiara, and my underwear, I preferred to leave early and change at the studio. This particular morning, however, I forgot that some rock star was filming a music video up on the deck I'd have to walk through.

Women packed the area from one railing to the next, forming an impenetrable wall. If I'd been wearing my pole shoes, I could've looked over them for some sort of path, but at my normal height, I was stuck.

"Excuse me!" I said. "Excuse me!"

Nothing. No response. After a moment, I turned to head back to the elevators. I could cross on a lower deck, then head back up. I met another woman's eyes on my way. "Giving up? We heard they might take a few more extras if people don't show."

"Oh, I'm not here for the video," I said. "I teach pole fitness."

"Really, here?"

"Yeah." I briefed her on the details while walking toward the elevator.

"Sounds cool," she said. "Maybe if my friends and I don't get in, we'll come up."

"Great! You can also come up after. Deck 15, next to the spa. Classes starting on the hour all morning, picking up again after lunch at one."

She thanked me when we reached the elevator bay. With another glance at the throng of people, I decided to take the stairs instead. Moments later, I darted into my studio, only four minutes late.

Luckily, the backup on the deck must've slowed everyone, because hardly anyone waited when I arrived. I changed quickly in the storeroom, and returned to find a group of about a dozen women, including the one I spoke to up on the deck. I waved at her.

"Good morning, everyone! My name is Janey." I paused with a practiced smile, making eye contact with each student in the front row before continuing my spiel. "This is where most pole fitness instructors will talk about how they're not strippers. I'm not going to do that. I used to be a stripper, and that's how I became damn good at working the pole."

A couple of the women gasped. Someone chuckled. I followed the sound to find an elderly black woman giving me the thumbs up. She received the real smile, not the practiced stage smile reserved for almost everyone.

Beaming back at me, she said, "Own it, girl."

I gave her a thumbs up before returning to the rest of the group. "Look, I'm not here to sugarcoat things. I'm here to teach you how to pole. I like dancing. I liked stripping; it paid well. I wasn't putting myself through law school or medical school or raising a bunch of sick orphans. It's just that I like to eat and pay my rent and stripping gave me the money to do those things. I'm not ashamed."

Some of the dubious looks started to fade, as usual. Occasionally at this point someone would leave, but most women who signed up for a pole fitness class on a cruise ship came to have fun and didn't care about the teacher's history. I'd never see most of them again. Except the ones who stayed back after class to read me the word of the Lord. That was always fun. I enjoyed explaining to people that you could believe in God and still be proud of the body he gave you and use it to your advantage. The Lord helps those who help themselves, right?

One woman sneered at me from the back of the room. It took me a minute to realize I recognized her. Her hair was pulled back in a messy bun and she wore no makeup this morning, but we'd met. In the boarding area, she was the woman who yanked Dr. Frank out of our conversation so he could board. Lila? Lena? No, Lisa. That's right. Even as my student, she wore the same disdainful expression most people reserved for stepping in dog poop. It took a lot of balls to glare at your teacher like that. With a deep breath, I forced myself to meet her eyes and smile. No reaction.

It didn't matter. I was here to teach a class, not make friends with snotty women. I wasn't allowed to toss students out of my classes unless they became physically or verbally abusive, so I might as well grin and bear it until the hour ended. After years of practice, not a problem.

To Lisa's right stood Frank, which made my smile widen a notch. Last night, I'd insisted that he attend as many of my regular classes as he could, but especially this first one. Before we could prepare for Saturday's show, I needed to assess his fitness level, strength, flexibility, and make sure he hadn't been lying about his ballet history. My first break in classes wasn't until three o'clock this afternoon, and I didn't want to lose half a day's planning and practice. Still, part of me was surprised he'd shown up, even after spotting Lisa. I wondered what he'd said to get her to come with him. Her body language told me Lisa didn't voluntarily sign up for an hour of pole fitness at seven a.m.

Most of the women in this room, including Lisa, wore running shorts or yoga pants (despite the program making it clear that the more skin exposed, the better) with tank tops. Frank had followed my directions, donning a pair of bicycle shorts that left nothing to the imagination. They clung so well to his thighs, I wanted to chastise him for wearing a longish shirt, brush that fabric aside to see how the spandex hugged his tight butt. From the day before I knew he had a nice body, but seeing it with my own eyes made me wipe my palms against my shorts.

Focus, Janey. Sweaty dancers don't stick to the pole. He's a means to an end.

"This class is about getting in touch with your inner self," I said. "Pole means something different to everyone. Some people use it to earn a living, like me. Some people like the confidence pole gives them. Some like to build their strength. And some women want to learn to be sexy."

While speaking, I never stopped moving around the pole. When I got to the word "confidence," I jumped up, locking my thighs around the pole. In the same seamless motion, I allowed myself to fall backwards and spread my arms wide, holding myself aloft by only my ankles. On "strong," I moved up, gripped the pole with my forearms, and lifted my legs straight out to one side like a flag blowing in the wind. And when I got to "sexy", I dropped to the floor, looking up at the others with a pouty face. By the time I finished, most of them were smiling. I didn't spare a glance for Lisa, but Frank looked impressed. When I met his eyes, he mimed enthusiastic clapping. Always playing to my audience, I gave him a sweeping bow.

A girl in the front row shook her head with a wry smile. When she moved her head, gorgeous blonde waves tumbled down her back. "I'm not sexy."

"That's BS," I said, and I meant it. Seeing this beautiful girl tell me she wasn't sexy made me want to throttle the society that said women all had to look like Pixie Stix. "What's your name?"

"Heidi."

"Well, Heidi, you have signed up for the sexy class. All of you have. Everyone can be sexy, once they give themselves permission. When you leave here, you will feel like the sexiest, fiercest bitch who ever walked a deck." She sucked her bottom lip between her teeth, but didn't contradict me. To the rest of the class, I said, "That reminds me–it's time to put on your shoes if you've got 'em. If not, there are spare pairs in the back of the room. Don't worry, I clean them after every use."

Once everyone changed into heels and returned to their poles, I reached up high and grabbed the pole beside me with my right hand. Using one arm, I swung around in a circle before kicking my legs out to swing in a scissor motion, circling around. With my left hand, I reached behind me and pushed off the pole, swinging my body back and forth while rotating around back to my starting point.

"Once you gain your confidence and master the basics, there's nothing you can't do. Is everyone ready?"

The women nodded. Heidi still looked dubious. Lisa looked a touch scared. I probably shouldn't have started off showing such complex moves; usually, I saved the real show for the end of the class. But seeing the look on her face, remembering the way she treated me for being "the help," made me want to show her that I was just as good as her. Putting that look of fear in her eyes made me smirk a bit on the inside, even knowing that sinking to Lisa's level didn't make me the better person.

We go high, I reminded myself, vowing to remain on my best behavior.

The class started with a fairly basic warm-up: squats and

stretches and leg lifts and sit-ups. Nothing too strenuous. On the fitness-themed cruises, I taught an entire class of just pole-related calisthenics, and it was killer. People moaned and groaned for days–but they also came back every morning at eight for more. But this week's cruise was largely for singles, meaning I taught sexy pole. At least it wasn't another Pets Onboard cruise. All those dogs in the pole room... I shuddered at the memory.

For these classes, I usually took it relatively easy on the group, starting with a few stretches and basic exercises to get everyone's heart rate up. But today, I needed to see what my new partner could do, so I pulled out all the stops.

By the time the warmup ended, most of the class panted for breath. Frank followed along smoothly, which eased my mind a bit. We didn't have time to build his stamina, so it helped that he started this project in good shape. He didn't have quite the flexibility I'd want for an advanced routine, but Penny and I could modify a couple of moves.

Then I showed the class the basics: walking around the pole, dipping and twirling, rocking our hips back and forth. Lisa moved mechanically, which didn't surprise me. That woman needed to learn to let go. Heidi, on the other hand, did great. Clearly better than she expected, judging by the smile on her face. And Cassandra, the woman who smiled at me early on, turned out to be the fiercest woman in the room. The way her hips wiggled back and forth as she moved around the pole taught me a thing or two about sassiness.

Finally, I'd worked my way around the entire class, ending with Frank. After the way my body reacted to seeing him in those shorts, the prudent thing to do was avoid him as long as possible. I didn't want to think about how I'd make it through our performance, which he would do bare-chested with me wearing a glittery bra top and booty shorts. Our bodies...No. I brushed the thought aside, forcing myself to remain professional.

"Hello, doctor," I said. "How are you enjoying the workout?"

"It's tough, but doable." He quirked an eyebrow at me as he glanced down my legs, gaze ending at my Pleasers. "I thought you were supposed to be taking it easy on your ankle."

"I am! It's all bandaged up, just like the doctor ordered."

"My instructions didn't include walking on stilts."

"Come on! These are only five inches," I said. "Besides, I'm so used to walking in heels, trying to move around flat-footed might make me more prone to injury."

"I doubt that," he said. "Just promise me to sit and elevate that ankle between classes."

"Yes, sir." His concern softened me toward him, but I reminded myself that he was a doctor. Clearly one with an excellent bedside manner, but nothing more.

Frank grinned at me. Over his shoulder, Lisa seethed silently. Not wanting to risk getting in trouble by pissing off a passenger friendly with both my boss and the owner's daughter, I switched back into instructor mode. "How are you doing with the basic chair spin?"

"Oh, it's no problem." With his right hand, Frank reached over his head, raising up onto his toes. He walked three steps before pulling so smoothly, I wouldn't have seen the muscles clench without looking for it. His legs came up off the floor, knees to his chest, while his left arm stretched across his body to rest on the pole. His body swung in a circle. If I'd had reason to doubt his dancer's background, those fears were immediately put to rest.

"No fair showing off!" Lisa said behind him. "We didn't all minor in dance."

Frank's face turned red as his toes came down to rest silently on the ground.

"It's fine," I said. "Pole is a great workout for all skill levels. Here, Lisa, let me give you a few tips."

To my surprise, she allowed me to help her. Once she relaxed, she improved dramatically.

"How do you move around the pole like that?" Lisa asked suddenly.

"What do you mean?"

"When you were showing us what you can do, at the beginning of class, you rotated around and around like it was nothing. Why weren't you screaming as all the skin ripped off your hand?"

"Actually, I wondered that, too," Frank said from off to our right. "The friction must be killer."

I reached out and grabbed the pole with one hand, twisting it the barest fraction of an inch in each direction. "These poles are locked. Mine isn't. For most of the complicated tricks, I'm not rotating around the pole. It's moving, and I go with it."

"Ahhh. So all you have to do is spot?" Frank asked.

More reassurance that he knew what he was doing. "Not exactly. The pole is the focal point, so you don't need to look into the distance. With some moves, we're spinning too fast to spot on anything. It's about practice."

Frank turned a bit green, and my stomach dropped.

I opened my mouth to reassure him, not even sure what I'd say without tipping Lisa off that our relationship went beyond "teacher and student for one class." She knew we'd met at the port, obviously, but not what happened since. If I had any say, it would stay that way, at least until the Talent Show.

Heidi called me from across the room, interrupting our conversation. I couldn't neglect my other students, so I went to her. She needed me to walk through the moves again, showing the proper points for applying pressure to the pole in order to achieve liftoff. Really basic stuff, and something I generally loved showing people. No one expected a pole fitness class to include a physics lesson.

I couldn't stop glancing at Frank behind my student's back. If he bailed, Penny and I would be in trouble. He refused to meet my gaze, staring at the pole as if it contained the secrets to the meaning of life. There was no way to tell if he was super focused or simply avoiding looking at me.

From the look in his eyes when I'd gone to help Heidi, I had a sinking feeling I knew the answer. He may be the one with the fancy, expensive education, but I'd learned plenty at the school of life. People who intended to help you didn't wear the expression on Frank's face for the rest of class.

At the end of the hour, I thanked everyone for attending. Briefly, I explained my availability until the end of the cruise and reminded them to return their shoes to the laundry basket in the corner. I stopped Heidi and her friends to see how they were doing and invite them to another class. It looked more natural when I talked to multiple students rather than making a beeline for Frank. Once they left, a couple of other women had questions.

Behind them, Lisa turned toward the door. A glance at her feet told me she'd brought her own heels. Pleasers made shoes in a variety of styles, heel heights, and colors, but I'd never seen anything like the shoes Lisa sported. That didn't surprise me. She didn't seem the type to wear borrowed footwear, even for a one-time exercise class.

My heart sank as I watched Frank file out of the room behind her. He didn't spare me a glance. The twisting in my gut told me he wasn't coming back.

CHAPTER FIVE

hroughout the rest of my morning classes, I kept an eye out for any promising student, anyone I might convince to help me out with the Talent Show finale. Maybe I'd get extremely lucky and National Pole Champion Carly Child would wander through the doors of my studio. Or maybe Penny's nausea would miraculously vanish.

Somehow, I suspected I'd have more luck trying to whip Cassandra into shape as my new partner than waiting for either of those events. Maybe she could sashay around while I flipped and spun.

Ugh. With a sigh, I flopped down onto the floor, stretching while I tried to summon the energy to go to lunch, where I'd have to tell Penny I scared away our only hope.

A voice broke the silence. "I'd offer a penny for your thoughts, but the way you're glaring at that pole makes me think you'd want at least a nickel."

My head shot up. Frank stood in the doorway, in the same t-shirt and shorts as earlier, grinning at me.

The sigh of relief that escaped me could have carried the

ship all the way to Jamaica. "I can't believe you're here. When you left, I thought you'd changed your mind."

He shook his head. "Have a little faith. Lisa wanted to talk to me, so I went with her to avoid arousing suspicions."

"You afraid to be seen with me?"

"I'm afraid that she'd hear why I'm dancing with you and say something to Max or Nellie. Did you want me to tell her?"

Oh, right. I unclenched my jaw. "Thank you. I'm sorry."

He reached out a hand, lifting me to my feet. "It's okay. I imagine I'd have the same concerns in your position. But I'm here to help. Where do we start?"

"The first step should probably be to show you the routine," I said. "But I worry about scaring you off."

"Isn't a partnership about trust?" Frank asked. "In ballet, if I don't trust my partner, I can overcompensate, use too much muscle, pull too hard, and seriously injure her."

He was right, and we both knew it. I felt ashamed for thinking about hiding the routine from him. Especially because I needed to know his weaknesses. Which moves terrified him? Which might we need to alter because he had a different body type than Penny? Better yet–where would I be able to push the routine, make it more difficult, enhance the doubles tricks in a way that showed off his strengths?

Taking a deep breath, I reached for the hem of my shirt and lifted it above my head.

Frank swallowed. "What are you doing?"

"Earlier today, you asked me about friction. We get it from skin on the pole. You and me both. There's a reason pole dancers typically only cover the areas absolutely necessary. It helps with the holds."

"Interesting," he said. "Does that mean I'm dancing without a shirt?"

Unfortunately. I'd spent an hour last night tossing and turning, trying to keep that very image out of my head. "It does. We need to toughen your skin this week. That reminds me..." I went to my gym bag in the corner and pulled out two oranges, which I tossed to him.

"You want me to juggle?"

"I want you to eat them."

"Thanks, but I'm not hungry. I'll grab something when we're done."

"You'll do that, too, but first, eat those," I said. "The Vitamin C helps prevent bruising. You don't want to walk around all week trying to explain to your sister why you've got a bunch of bruises on places like the tops of your feet or your armpits."

He blinked several times. "Bruises...armpits?"

"We call 'em pole kisses," I said. "Once you get used to the pole, you won't get them, but we don't have time. For now, an orange before and after each session. If a bruise appears, rub butter on it before bed, then sprinkle it with salt and cover up with good, thick socks."

"Turning me into a baked potato isn't going to reduce bruising," he said. "That's not how science works. You're trying to make me look ridiculous."

"I wish," I said. "It's a real thing."

The look on his face clearly conveyed that he didn't believe me, but it wasn't worth arguing. Tomorrow morning, he'd have a different point of view. For now, we'd spent enough time talking. Telling him about pole, even talking about the routine, wouldn't have nearly as powerful an effect as showing him.

I strode to the stereo system in the corner and pulled up a song. Then I pulled my hair back, shook out my arms, and tossed him the remote. "When I give you the signal, press play."

The routine started with Penny and me–that is, Frank and me–lying on the ground, each curled in a ball around a separate pole. I got into the position and raised my arm, counting to three with my fingers. A moment later, the opening notes of *(I've Had) the Time of My Life* filled the room. I'd shortened the song for the performance, since the original clocked in at nearly five minutes.

Slowly, I stretched in time with the music, laying out on my back, then rolling over, sitting up, and grabbing the pole. With a leg swing, suddenly I spun up the pole, legs stretched in a vee on either side. With the click of my heels, I landed on my feet before the music tempo increased and I threw myself into the heart of the routine. Kicking, spinning, twisting, jumping. Back and forth from one pole to the next. When I got to the parts that required the two of us to work together, I modified the moves to give him the idea. Three minutes later, the music faded away as I lowered myself to the ground, once again curling into a ball around the pole.

Then I popped up, turning toward my audience with a bow, anxious to see his reaction. I'd tried sneaking peeks here and there during the performance, but pole didn't work that way. Not for me. I practiced each routine endlessly until the movements came as naturally as breathing. Once the opening notes filled the room, the music carried me into an almost trancelike state. I barely had any awareness of the world around me until I finished. The *Aphrodite* could've hit an iceberg without me noticing.

Frank watched me, eyes wide, still as stone. I could've knocked him over with a feather. But the expression didn't seem like fear at what he would be expected to do in a few short days. No, unless I misread him, the emotion covering his face was... awe. As I stared, he came alive, clapping slowly at first, then with enthusiasm.

"I've never seen anyone look so alive," he said. "I know you thought I'd be scared by the difficulty, but I want to feel the way you look. I'm in, one hundred percent."

After my demonstration, we parted for lunch. Pole burned a lot of calories, and while I could get through a morning of beginner classes without doing anything too strenuous, Frank and I would be working hard all afternoon. I sent him to the dining room with instructions to eat as if he had a long day of ballet practice coming up, then come on back.

Since we couldn't arrive at the studio together and I really did have my own training to work on, I downed two meat-loaded slices of pizza up on deck, then went back twenty minutes before our scheduled meeting. After refilling my water bottle plus a spare for my partner, I changed into my workout clothes and started stretching. Soon, my warm-up music filled the air and I dipped, spun, and swung.

When the music stopped, clapping filled the air, startling me. After so many years of dancing to a chorus of hooting and hollering in the clubs, my grip didn't slip even a centimeter. I simply lowered myself to the ground and turned toward Frank's appreciative gaze with an exaggerated bow.

"Wow," he said when I straightened, looking up the length of the pole at the ten-foot ceilings before returning his gaze to my sports bra and booty shorts. I shivered, and not just from the cool ocean air against my exposed skin. "I know you showed me the routine earlier, but seeing you let yourself go like that? It's amazing."

His words made me flush with pride. So many people looked down on my job. I pretended not to care, but it meant a lot to hear someone appreciate my hard work. "Thanks. How long have you been watching?"

"Not long," he said. "Can you show me another trick?"

"I plan to show you lots of tricks."

The words were out of my mouth before I caught the double

meaning. Frank got it, though. His grin sent a jolt through me, reminding me that no matter how much I lied to myself, I had it bad for this guy. "I meant the really advanced stuff."

With a nervous cough, I said, "We should start with the basics. You got a good base in class this morning with the chair spin and the climb, but there's so much more."

"We'll get to all that, but watching you is inspiring. Just one move. I still can't believe you climb that thing while it's spinning."

"It's easier than it looks. Stand back." I reached for the pole with my right hand, then placed my right shin bone along the length of the metal, knee on one side, ankle to the other. With a small tug, my left leg left the ground, swinging smoothly in an arc before wrapping around the pole to meet my other leg. As I moved, the momentum from my swinging leg brought the pole around in a smooth circle, turning me back around to face Frank.

"That's awesome," he said.

"You'll be doing it yourself by the end of the day. You remember me mentioning physics this morning?"

"Yeah. Why?"

"Pole has three key elements: push, pull, and momentum. Every move needs all three. For example, in the swing we did this morning, your momentum comes from the steps. You *pull* with your upper hand while *pushing* against the metal with the hand across your body. Push, pull, momentum. There's a bit of geometry, too. We're largely making triangles. But start with the physics."

"Push, pull, momentum," he repeated. "When you put it like that, it sounds easy. How does it work in practice?"

"Like this." I reached up the pole again with my left hand, high above my head. My legs pressed against the pole. "Push." I yanked with my hand. "Pull," then scooted my legs up the metal rod. "Momentum." Then I repeated the motion until I'd climbed to the ceiling. "See?"

Frank let out a whistle. "You're like Spiderman!"

"You ain't seen nothing yet." Holding myself aloft with my grip, I unwrapped my legs and swung them upward. My outside knee locked around the metal, and my inside leg fell back, the weight holding me in place. My torso fell backward, and m y arms spread out as if to say, "ta-da!"

"A little warning next time, please. I thought you were going to crack your head open. Your legs must be very strong."

"The better to hold you with," I said without thinking. Since I was hanging upside, all the blood had already rushed to my face, or I'd have turned purple. The air around us sizzled, which would never do. We needed to keep things professional. In an effort to lighten the mood, I said, "Spiderman never falls."

He approached, and our eyes locked. His dilating pupils made me want to go limp, sag against him. Sternly, I reminded myself to keep my leg on the pole, or this trick would end in disaster. "I guess that makes me Mary Jane."

With a start, I remembered the scene he was talking about. In one of the movies, Spiderman hangs upside down, and Mary Jane moves his mask enough to kiss him. Frank's lips were at the perfect height to recreate that moment. I could stop him. I could release my grip enough to slide down and place my arms on the ground, then kick over. Or crunch my abs up, taking myself out of his range. Desire froze me in place. It was such a bad idea, but my lips tingled at the thought of Frank kissing me.

Someone coughed. It wasn't me. I jerked my gaze away from Frank's luscious mouth to find Penny standing in the doorway. "Hey, guys."

"What are you doing here?" I asked, trying not to sound annoyed. In all honesty, she'd saved me from making a huge mistake. I needed to get ahold of myself.

"I'm here to help," she said. "As much as I can while leaning against a wall and trying not to puke."

"There's a mop bucket in the corner," I offered helpfully. She gave me a weak smile.

"Actually, I'm glad you're here," Frank said. "I was planning to check on you later. I've got something for you."

"A gift?"

"Not exactly. Well, sort of. You mentioned trying to get pills to help with the nausea, but they were too expensive?"

"Oh, I can't accept that from you," Penny said quickly. "They cost way too much."

"Yes, they do," Frank agreed. "But a little known secret? The active ingredients are anti-nausea drugs and a vitamin. Each costs less than five dollars for over a hundred, and each is free to passengers. I stopped by the infirmary before lunch and got a bottle of each for you."

Penny's face lit up so much, I thought she might have fallen in love with Frank on the spot. Who could blame her? "Thank you. Really."

"It was my pleasure. I hate thinking that it's so hard for people to get medical care. This was an easy problem for me to solve."

"Still." I lowered myself to the ground, practically dizzy with gratitude. "You didn't have to do that. Most people wouldn't have bothered."

"I'm not most people."

"No," I said, thinking about the way he moved, the heat smoldering his eyes, the fact that he was spending half his cruise vacation doing us a favor. "You're really not."

CHAPTER SIX

DAY THREE: JAMAICA

The third day of our voyage, my practice sessions with Frank hit an unexpected snag. My boss stopped me and Penny at the door to my studio after breakfast. "You can't go in there. Ferret problem."

"I'm sorry, Max, what?" I couldn't believe my ears.

"You heard me right. There's a loose ferret in the walls."

"Oh no." Penny groaned. "Another one of Lincoln's bright ideas?"

"I don't think so," Max said. "The powers that be were pretty clear that the Pets Onboard cruise was a one-time experiment, and it failed."

Last one, one of the assistant cruise directors tried to spice things up, with disastrous results. Those of us who found ourselves chasing pets and stopping dogs from "marking" the poles were not eager to repeat the experiment. I was relieved to hear that upper management agreed.

"So what happened?" I asked.

He shook his head. "I don't even know. Some passenger must have smuggled it onto the ship back in Miami. The darn thing's been turning up everywhere. Yesterday, it ran across some poor woman's legs while she was sleeping at the pool."

"And it's really a ferret? Not, like, a small dog?" I asked. "Are you sure it's not a service animal?"

"You ever hear of a service ferret?" Max didn't wait for me to reply. "Anyway, for now, no lessons. We've got to open up the wall behind that mirror to find it."

The news kicked me in the chest. I couldn't afford to lose the entire morning. Not when we only had a few days for Frank to learn the routine. Cancelling my classes should have made me ecstatic, since it gave me extra time to practice. But until they caught the ferret and fixed the wall, we didn't have anywhere to go. The ship didn't have many random poles for twirling on.

With a heavy heart, I sent Penny to relax in our cabin while I waited for Frank. There was no point in her hanging around to help with a cancelled session. When my new partner appeared outside the entrance to the spa, I pulled him toward the ship's railing, away from anyone who might overhear us. I pasted a huge smile on my face so anyone who saw us chatting would think we had a perfectly normal entertainer/passenger conversation.

"Why do you look so happy?" Frank asked. "This is terrible news."

Without faltering, I explained. He plastered on a similarly forced smile, so fake, I burst out laughing. The sound carried out across the ocean. It felt good to let some of my stress out, so I laughed harder. And harder, until I doubled over, clutching the railing.

By the time I composed myself, Frank stared at me as if contemplating the likelihood that I had experienced a psychotic break and might push him into the sea. "Sorry. It's been a long couple of days. I'm tired, stressed, and a bit punchy. Sometimes all you can do is laugh."

He nodded. "I get it. When things get really rough, I can't function. Have to sit on the floor and listen to Tchaikovsky until I feel better."

For a moment, an image flitted before my eyes. Me and Frank, sitting on the ground together, listening to classical music. Kissing.

I forced myself to shake it away. We were dance partners, and maybe becoming friends, but that's all this could ever be. "Thanks for understanding. Sorry our plans are ruined."

"Maybe it's not the end of the world," he said. "I've got bruises everywhere."

"You didn't try the butter and salt?"

"Of course not. I figured you were joking."

I grinned at him. "Nope. An old wives' tale, but something in the butter reduces swelling. It absolutely works. Try it tonight before you get in bed. At least you won't get new bruises."

"There's no possible way that's going to work," he said. "But since you mentioned it—We can practice in my cabin. I've got a suite."

"A suite? Fancy!"

He shrugged. "My sister talked me into rooms with adjacent balconies. She wanted to be able to sit out in the sun without anyone else around."

Must be nice to have so much money you'd pay extra to sit around by yourself after spending thousands to vacation with a literal boatload of other people. Apparently it wasn't peaceful enough on the gorgeous decks or near the pools.

When I first got this job, I looked online to see what the different rooms cost. The price of one of the highest-level suites for one week would have paid my dad's care for two months, and things had only gotten more expensive since then.

He tilted his head at me if noting my increased tension. "What? What's wrong?"

"Just wondering if there will be enough space," I lied. The way he read my body cues freaked me out. "But if nothing else, we can stretch and do handstands against the wall. You need to practice. Lead the way."

When we reached his room, Frank stopped talking and scowled. It was on the tip of my tongue to ask what was wrong when he started patting his pockets, the universal symbol for "Where are my keys?"

He answered my unspoken question. "When I got up for breakfast, I put on my workout clothes. Meant to slip my key card in my shorts, but then Lisa messaged to tell me about this guy she met last night after I slipped away to practice." He sighed. "I guess we'll have to go to reception and get another one."

I couldn't wait in the reception line with him, but riding the elevator together shouldn't raise any suspicions. Unfortunately, when we got downstairs, the line of people waiting snaked around the room and only two concierges worked at the front. They tapped frantically at their screens while my heart plummeted. We didn't have a lot of time, and we couldn't afford to spend half of it standing here.

Frank nudged my elbow with his. It probably wasn't supposed to be an intimate gesture, but still sent a thrill up my arm. "I don't think I'm the only one who got locked out this morning."

Maybe we could go somewhere else. My cabin was out. This time of day, the corridors would be swarming with entertainers. We couldn't risk being noticed by the wrong person. Also, Penny was in bed, resting up before the afternoon Bingo session. Drawing numbers and reading them out while sitting in a chair was one of the few things she could do without getting dizzy. Hopefully the pills Frank got her would help, but we didn't know yet. Not to mention, our cabin was tiny. Nothing like having an entire suite to move around in.

The only time I'd ever gotten a peek inside those cabins was during my first week on the ship, when Robbie offered me a tour before the passengers finished boarding. Too late, I realized his intent to impress me with the luxury of the upscale cabins in order to seduce me. He'd heard a lot about pole dancers, apparently, but not how strong we were.

Too bad he'd learned to finesse his act significantly before I thought to warn Penny about him. But as I remembered that day, my brain zeroed in on an important feature of the executive class suites.

"Is your balcony door locked?" I asked.

He shrugged. "Not unless it locks automatically when you close the door. I was out there last night."

A very, very bad idea was forming in my head. The rational side of my brain told me to give up, stop talking, and walk away. The part of me that needed time alone with Frank to go over everything–where there was no possibility of Max or anyone else finding us–continued talking. "Then it's not. The latch is near the ceiling. You'd know if you locked it."

He narrowed his eyes at me. "Why do you mention this?"

"Because I've got a way to get into your room."

"No. Uh-uh. I know I agreed to help, but I'm not scaling the side of the ship for you. This won't take long." He strode away from me, toward the back of the line. I kept in step with him easily.

At that moment, the woman at one of the kiosks in the front picked up her microphone. "Attention, ladies and gentlemen. I do apologize, but it appears that our systems are currently unavailable. We expect them to come back up within about an hour." She continued, listing things they could do without a system, but I tuned her out. Replacement key cards wasn't one of those things.

Frank sighed. "You win. What now?"

I couldn't exactly take a passenger's hand and lead him through the ship. "Meet me on the observation deck. You take the elevator."

"What about you?"

"I'll take the stairs."

"In those shoes?" He gestured at my ever-present high heels. This pair had black platform and stilettos, with red bows on the ankle and toe straps. They were sexy as hell, if I did say so myself. Which I did, at least to my dancer friends.

I grinned at him. "Yup."

Scaling the side of the ship wasn't what I had in mind, but Frank might prefer that option when he figured out my plan. Now to beat him to the back of the observation deck. Luckily, the elevators moved slowly with so many people, and I knew the shortcuts. I had at least three minutes to consider the stupidity of my plan before Frank arrived.

He stopped and leaned on the railing beside me. "Now what?"

I pointed up. "Your balcony is right up there."

"Yes, I know. How do we get to it?"

The observation deck was supported by a line of poles, each about fifteen feet high and fifty millimeters wide. The tops of the poles attached only a few inches away from the edge of the floor above. "We climb, of course. Quickly, without anyone seeing us."

"You must have banged your head on the pole one too many times," Frank said. "No way I can do this."

"You've already done this at least a dozen times," I pointed out.

"I've been doing it in a studio, over mats. Where a fall means a bruised ego, not death."

"You haven't fallen once. Come on. I'm not asking you to try a fonji." The move I mentioned was extremely difficult, where the dancer let go of the pole and flipped over in mid-air before grabbing it again. I'd scrapped it from the routine when Frank stepped in, because there simply wasn't time to teach him.

"There's no way."

"Fine," I said. "Don't take my word for it."

I couldn't afford to spend the next twenty minutes arguing. Every second ticking by made it more likely someone would come looking for me, or that another guest would brave the winds to take in the view. If anyone caught me helping a guest break into his room, I'd be fired faster than a project manager on *The Apprentice* who accepted blame for poor leadership.

Instead of continuing the discussion, I walked to the pole on my left. Frank's room lay on the back corner of the ship, twelfth deck. The eleventh level housed the observation deck, a daycare that wouldn't open for another hour, and an executive lounge people could use throughout the day. This was our only chance. With single-minded determination, I grabbed onto the pole high above my head, using both hands to circle it. Then I braced one leg on the pole just the way I showed my students, pushed with my right leg, and pulled with my hands. My left leg came off the floor and gripped the pole, holding me fast.

"See? Easy-peasy."

He let out a sigh. "Fine. You win."

I dropped to the ground. "You first. I'm right behind you."

"What happens when I get to the top?"

I pointed. "The top of the post is attached to the roof, which is also the floor of your balcony. Grip with your legs. Feel with one hand at a time around the edge until you find the balcony rails. It'll be like a ladder. Reach as high as you can, pull with both hands, and bring your legs up."

"You make it sound so easy. As if I won't die if I mess it up."

"Oh, you will." I grinned at him. "So don't."

"Thanks for the pep talk."

"I have faith in you."

He grabbed the pole and inched upward, much as I had done. I gazed around the deck, grateful for the rain clouds that kept most people inside this morning. Still, once breakfast ended, anyone might wander down here to look at the water. We needed to hurry, but the look on Frank's face told me not to push it.

Instead, I waited for him to get about seven feet off the ground, then grabbed the pole and hoisted myself up again. "You're doing great. I'm right here. I won't let you fall."

In response, he grunted and continued his upward movement. Luckily, I'd climbed enough to continue the motions while keeping one eye on my student and the other on the hallway.

Footsteps sounded down the deck.

"Someone's coming!" I hissed.

"I'm doing the best I can."

Voices carried on the wind to my ears. I froze, torn between sliding to the ground and shoving Frank the rest of the way. Then the footsteps stopped. "Go! Go!"

He reached the top and felt around the sides of the ship for the bottom railing of his balcony. This was the riskiest part. The sun shone behind us, waiting to blind anyone who looked up. If someone saw us, they might assume their eyes were playing tricks. More importantly, the way the balconies were tiered, no one should be able to see anything-except for those few seconds when we'd be hanging out between decks, on the outside of the ship. Luckily, most passengers should be on the other side, taking pictures and getting ready to explore Jamaica.

The footsteps started again. Two pairs. Then a third, much faster. A voice. "Stop!"

My heart skipped a beat. I wiped sweaty palms on my shorts while sparing a glance down the hall. From my angle, I could just make out two pairs of feet, both pointed toward the other end of the ship. They must have stopped to talk to whoever ran toward them.

Above me, Frank's shoes scraped across the railing. He vanished, and a thud sounded over my head. Praise Jesus, he'd made it.

Once he entered his room, he could open the door from the inside to let me in. But I'd come this far, and I wanted him to see that I wasn't afraid to do the same things I asked of him. I also didn't want anyone to see me wandering the halls near the passenger suites, where I had no reason to be. More importantly, at the moment, if I slid down the pole, I'd get caught.

I didn't waste another second. As the footsteps started toward us again, I scrambled upward. My right hand closed around the railing outside Frank's balcony, and my left hand found the next rung. Stretching as far as I could, I gripped the railing for dear life before letting go of the pole with my legs.

The voices continued, and this time I recognized them. Repugnant Robbie, talking to some poor girl. Not Penny, a mixed blessing. I felt bad that she fell for such a creep, but if he was talking to some other girl, he wasn't messing with my friend's emotions.

My legs still hung in the air between the decks. I froze, praying they didn't look up, because they couldn't miss me. With agonizing slowness, I inched my knees toward my chest, getting my feet out of their line of sight. I couldn't risk the big move-ment that would take me over the railing. Robbie would call

Max in a heartbeat. Ever since I told Penny the truth about him, Robbie had it in for me.

The woman's voice drifted to my ears. "I could've sworn I saw Frank walking this way."

With a start, I realized that I recognized her voice, too. Lisa. With all my heart, I hoped Robbie wasn't the "cute guy" she told Frank about meeting, and that she'd just stopped a random member of the staff to ask for directions.

No such luck. Robbie said something, too low for my ears to pick up, and Lisa giggled. A very flirtatious sound, not "thanks for the help, stranger."

Frank's face appeared over the railing, jarring me from my thoughts. He motioned with one hand, and I saw that my feet had crept as high as the floor of the balcony. Thank goodness, because my abs were screaming. I stepped onto the solid floor, then pulled myself upright, still moving slowly. Robbie and Lisa sounded otherwise occupied (gag!) but I still didn't want to catch their attention.

Someone needed to warn Lisa, as awful as she was, but I couldn't be the one to do it. Not here, for one thing. I also hadn't forgotten the way Lisa treated me when we met. She didn't seem likely to accept life advice from "the help," and I certainly wasn't going to tell her what Robbie did to Penny. Once we got upstairs, I'd let Frank know what I'd seen and hope Lisa would listen to her little brother. With dozens of Sassy Singles aboard this ship, surely, she could do better.

Thinking about Lisa's love life wasn't going to get me to my destination, though, and I couldn't afford to be distracted. Finally, I pulled myself high enough to swing one leg over the railing. I stepped lightly, although part of me wanted to thump loudly. Maybe I could scare Lisa into running away, certain that the ship was haunted.

Frank's arms locked around me, and he swept me off my feet.

A thrill shot through my entire body as the momentum caused me to press up against him. We spun in a circle. His lips nearly touched my ear, making me shiver as he spoke. "You're wild."

His peal of laughter was so infectious, I joined him, the sound flying out to sea. "What?"

"You're WIIIIILLLLLD!"

CHAPTER SEVEN

It had been months since I glimpsed any of the suites. What I'd seen didn't prepare me for the sight of Frank's cabin. Even the balcony was nice, with soft-looking lounge chairs and a dining set facing out to sea. Curious, I reached over and shook one of the chairs. As I thought, bolted to the deck.

"You coming?" Frank asked from the open doorway.

"Yeah. Sorry." I shook myself, but took two steps before stopping dead. "Wow."

Before me lay the nicest room I'd ever seen. Thick, plush carpet covered the floors. Penny and I had cheap carpet with one of those floral prints that hid stains. Frank's floor was a deep gray. The bed took up most of the left side of the room, with massive throw pillows lined across it. No towel animal, so housekeeping hadn't been by yet. I noted with amusement that he'd stopped to make the bed before meeting me. Of course he had. Frank was probably the type who did hospital corners. Over the windows and glass doors hung the kind of drapes made of such luxurious, heavy cloth, you understand why someone might make a dress out of them. Large sashes held them open to let sunlight into the space, but I suspected the cabin would be as dark as my windowless room if we closed them. The curtains probably cost more than all my furniture.

To the right was a sofa, coffee table, and armchair, a living room as big as the one in my dad's apartment where I grew up. There wasn't a piece of clothing or suitcase in sight. "Where's all your stuff?"

"In the drawers."

"Really?"

"Yeah. I like to feel at home, so I always unpack as soon as I arrive in a hotel room."

Having never stayed anywhere other than a fleabag motel for a couple of weeks after we got evicted over my twelfth birthday, I didn't know how to respond to that. "Okay. Let's go over the steps."

Luckily, the space between the bed and the living area allowed me to demonstrate the floor work we'd be doing with the routine. Then we used the walls to practice headstands. It wasn't the perfect practice area, but I put Frank through the motions. Before long, he was sweating.

After a couple of hours, we stopped for a break. I filled two glasses of water from the pitcher on the bathroom vanity and joined Frank on the couch.

"You're still in great shape," I said. "When did you quit ballet?"

"During my junior year of college. A drunk driver ran a red light and hit me while I was walking home one night."

A chill went down my spine at how close he'd come to getting killed. I put one hand on his knee. "That's awful. I'm so sorry."

"Thanks. All things considered, I was very lucky. Broke both legs and my wrist." He paused. "I don't talk about it much."

"Sorry to bring up a painful subject."

"It's okay," he said. "I was good, but I'd long suspected I didn't have the fire to make a career out of it. My parents made a very generous donation to get me into my school's ballet program. Besides, after that, I got interested in sports injuries and sports medicine, and here we are."

"Good thing you did, or who would have taped up my ankle?"

"Exactly! It was kismet." He glanced at me. I became very aware of my hand, still resting on his leg. He swallowed, and his pupils dilated. If I leaned in, our lips would touch. I wanted it so badly, but I couldn't. The realization made me shift backward. If he touched me, I'd be as lost as Penny, still stuck on a man she'd never have a future with.

After a moment, Frank cleared his throat awkwardly. "What about you? How did you get into pole?"

"We grew up poor," I said. "Me and my sister. And not like 'well, we'll keep the car for a couple of extra years before trading it in.' Real poor. When tuna went on sale for ten cents a can, Dad used his last dollar to stock up and then we rationed it until payday. We didn't go to the dentist, ever. We didn't have a car, and we lined our shoes with cardboard found behind grocery stores to hide the holes."

He flushed, reminding me that everything about this guy screamed money. I'd certainly never dreamed of medical school or owning an Apple watch or...taking a vacation.

"That must have been rough," he said.

"Sometimes. Mostly, I didn't know how bad it was. Heather and I were kids, going to school and doing homework and playing make believe games. But then, someone would show up in class with the newest tech or an expensive doll, and all I could think was how many meals it would have bought. Or the PTA mom would ask everyone to donate five dollars to buy a gift for the teacher, and I'd pretend to be sick that day because I couldn't get the money. It wasn't even worth asking Dad, because it wasn't there."

A lump formed in my throat at the memory, and I gazed down at my fingernails. Most people didn't get it, couldn't comprehend what it was like not to be able to find an extra few bucks. I didn't want to see the pity in his eyes.

"I'm sorry." He touched my wrist, held it until I looked up at him. To my surprise, his eyes weren't full of pity–or worse, laughter. "That must've been difficult for a kid."

"Thanks. It is what it is. Anyway, I dropped out of school when I was sixteen to get a job. Worked at the grocery store, the mall, the food court. Everything paid crap. Then one day, this older guy I was seeing took me to the local strip club. Used my sister's ID to get in, although it turned out they didn't card me."

Frank chuckled. "Yeah, most of those places are glad if women show up at all."

I continued as if he hadn't said anything. "When I saw those dancers up on stage, it was intoxicating. First of all, the men were throwing money at them like it meant nothing. But then they brought out a pole, and this woman started flying around it. So beautiful, so graceful. More than anything, I wanted to do what she did."

"I know that feeling."

Of course he did. "The next day, I went back and waited outside for her. She wasn't there, so I went back every day after work until she showed up. Told her how much I enjoyed watching her perform and asked her to teach me. She didn't have a studio, so the only way I could learn was to get hired."

"You were sixteen?"

"Yeah, but I still had my sister's ID. And everyone uses stage names, so it didn't matter that mine didn't match."

"What was your stage name?" I hesitated, and he smacked

himself on the forehead. "Oh. Janey, right? I can't believe I don't even know your real name."

A small smile crossed my lips. "My real name is Jane. Plain Jane."

"You're anything but plain," he said.

The compliment made my entire body feel lighter, but I played it cool. "You're not so bad yourself."

"Then what? You got the job."

"Yup. The boss gave me three days to watch and learn, serving drinks before taking the stage. From then on, I was on my own."

"Trial by fire, huh?"

"Pretty much." I smiled at him. "The other dancers helped. At first, I was scared and awkward. But then the men started responding to me. The more tricks I learned, the more they cheered. After a few months, I got good enough to dance on the weekends, then to headline. By the time I turned eighteen, this guy from another club approached me. Real classy place. Offered me a thousand dollar bonus to come work for him."

"Nice."

"It was like day and night. Where the first club was dingy, a little dark, this place had spotlights, a cover charge, private dances...Suddenly, instead of collecting ones and fives, I've got men stuffing hundred dollar bills into my panties. Offering me jewelry, cars, everything I ever wanted."

"Sounds like a dream." His tone gave nothing away.

I leaned back against the couch, allowing myself to sink into the fabric. "I know it's not most people's dreams. A lot of people look down on me for doing what I do. But I loved it. I loved the empowerment that comes from knowing every eye in the room is on me. That men would pay thousands of dollars to sleep with me."

"I wasn't being sarcastic. I really meant, growing up so poor, you were living a dream."

"Thanks." I paused. "I never did, you know. Sleep with any of them. Some of the other dancers did, but I made enough stripping."

"It wouldn't matter," he said. "It's none of my business."

I didn't know if he meant it wasn't his business because he didn't care about my past or because he didn't care about me as a person. I couldn't bring myself to ask. Not now. We had four more days together. Then the ship would dock back in Miami. I'd move on to Seattle to join the Alaskan cruises for the next few months, and he'd.... do things with Nellie that made my stomach clench.

"What happened?" he asked, breaking into my thoughts. "After that fancy club, what brought you here?"

"Heather found out," I said. "She got audited by the IRS for not reporting earnings she didn't know she had. Told me that she'd tell our father if I didn't stop. It sounds silly, I know, since I was an adult by then, but part of me couldn't stand to see the disappointment in Dad's eyes. So I started looking for 'respectable' dancing jobs."

"And here you are."

"Here I am. Making less than half what I got before, pouring my heart out like some fool, complaining about my sister."

"You're not a fool," he said. "People who trust their partners dance better together. This is important. Are you glad she caught you?"

"It is what it is," I said. "She's older than me. Things weren't as bad when she lived at home, before Dad got sick. She finished high school, went to community college, and moved out by the time I was fifteen. Dad and I were both so proud, we never wanted Heather to know how bad things got once he couldn't work. The bills kept piling up, but we didn't want to ask her for help. I always wonder what would have happened if we'd been closer in age."

"Let me tell you, being the same age as your siblings isn't all it's cracked up to be," he said. "That just makes it easy for them to cause trouble and blame it on you."

"Yeah, maybe. Maybe it wouldn't have been any better."

Frank leaned over and took my hand in his. I put my head on his shoulder, grateful for the few minutes of peace before the studio reopened and we had to re-enter the real world.

For the most part, cruise liners shut down while the ship was in port. They did this to encourage travelers to go ashore and contribute to the local economies of the places we visited. Members of the entertainment staff who didn't also work in housekeeping or laundry didn't have a lot to do between breakfast and dinner. Usually, I offered one-on-one classes by appointment, but my schedule for Wednesday was relatively clear.

Penny drew the job of herding people to their pre-purchased excursions, so we went to breakfast together. Beneath the layers of makeup, her face was white, but thanks to the pills, she managed to pull herself together enough to handle the job. Most average cruise-goers wouldn't notice the pallor beneath her naturally brown complexion or that she'd lost weight, even as her breasts grew larger.

Meanwhile, I snarfed my breakfast so I could sneak off to the studio before Max asked me to do something like ride the ferries back and forth from the ship to the dock all day. Ordinarily, I loved that job, but today Frank and I needed to practice. Max would be suspicious if I turned down the opportunity, so it was better to avoid him.

Frank needed to spend part of the day in port with Lisa and his friends so they didn't start asking questions. In the back of my mind, I knew he'd been spending time with Nellie over the course of the cruise–Penny saw them together while she handed out answer sheets at trivia one night. He couldn't abandon his entire vacation, and I couldn't ask him to do more than the daily practices. But we agreed to spend the morning going over the routine while his friends explored Grand Cayman, and he promised to talk to Lisa about Robbie before meeting me.

As usual, my pre-breakfast "Find Your Inner Diva" class was packed with travelers who wanted to get in a workout before spending the day exploring the island. I thrilled at getting to work with all of these women, show them some moves, and hopefully inspire them to take a class or two after returning home.

When class ended, I hung back as usual, stretching and going over the routine in my mind. A few students came up to ask follow-up questions and get pointers, and I welcomed the distraction to keep me from thinking about my growing crush on my new pole partner. Frank would be here soon enough, and all I could think about was the way he almost kissed me our first time alone in this very room. My pulse raced, thinking of the possibilities on a mostly-deserted ship. Which could never happen.

For the thousandth time, I reminded myself that he was only doing me a favor, that Frank was dating Nellie, that stealing the owner's daughter's boyfriend would get me fired, and that he was way, way out of my league. Chemistry between dancers on stage translated to an amazing performance. Chemistry off-stage would result in disaster. Better to keep my distance.

Before Frank arrived, I pulled my warm-up clothes back on,

looking to add any barrier between us. He didn't need me to demo most of the moves anymore. I could issue directions without getting too close.

He showed up right on time, as usual. "Hey."

"Hey! How are the bruises this morning?"

"Lisa caught me rubbing butter on my feet last night." He glared at me when I giggled. "Now she thinks I'm into something kinky. I don't want to talk about it."

"And your feet?"

He sighed. "No new bruises. I refuse to admit you were right about this, so now I immediately change the subject. How's Penny?"

"She seemed better this morning. She'll be here soon, so you can ask her yourself."

"Excellent!" He rubbed his hands together, then stretched his arms over his head, one wrist pulling the other. The hem of his shirt followed, revealing a couple of inches of gorgeous tanned skin.

I forced myself to look away. "Yeah. Are you ready?"

"Aye, aye, Captain." He saluted, which made me laugh.

We went through our stretches quickly, Frank having taken a run around the upper track during my class to jump start our workout. Then I walked him through the moves, starting with the most basic. Once he mastered the easy stuff, we'd go over the more difficult positions. He had the strength, the balance, the grace. Now he needed the confidence.

After the last early morning traveler disembarked for their excursions, Penny joined us. Her face was flushed for the first time in ages, and she wore a bright, real smile rather than the showgirl smile reserved for guests. "I did it! Rode back and forth and back and forth and didn't feel sick at all. Frank, you're a genius!"

"I'm not a genius, I'm a doctor," he said. "Anyone in my position would have helped you. I'm just glad it worked. If you had HG, you'd have to be hospitalized and given fluids; the pills wouldn't have helped. Looks like just a bad case of morning sickness."

"Thank goodness," I said.

"With that said, if it doesn't stay better, you need to schedule an examination," Frank said. "Immediately. I understand your situation, but you could be putting yourself and the baby at risk."

"Don't rain on my parade," Penny said. "I feel great, and I want to see what I can do."

She whipped off her shirt and pants, leaving a hot pink sports bra and black booty shorts. Frank barely glanced at her, which didn't escape my notice. Then she leaned down and touched the floor, bouncing from one side to the other before dropping to the ground and continuing to stretch.

"Does this mean you're back? You don't need Frank to do the routine?" I held my breath waiting for her answer.

On the one hand, we'd worked so hard, it would be a shame for Frank not to be able to show off what he'd learned. On the other hand, we'd only been practicing a few days, we had a long way to go, and not much time to get there. Penny knew the routine cold.

If some part of me wasn't ready to say good-bye to Frank, I refused to acknowledge it. Everything would be better for both of us if he walked out that door and never looked back. My heart would recover.

"One thing at a time," she said. "Right now, I'm here to help. I thought we could go through the routine so Frank can see how it looks with doubles. Then, he and I can do it so you can see his weak spots."

"And then you'll watch the two of us?" She nodded. Perfect. A perfect plan.

"That would be great," Frank said. "Janey's explained every-thing, but I need to see it."

I changed quickly, and the two of us took our places. Frank pressed the button to start the music, and the familiar notes entered my consciousness. Stretch, sit up, swing. Climb. Twist, swing, drop. Penny moved a bit slower than usual, but every move felt right. I'd missed this. Dancing for the love of the dance, doing what I did best–without a hot, dancing doctor constantly making me wish passengers weren't off-limits.

Lost in the moment, I didn't notice that Penny stopped until Frank raced by me. My friend stood gripping her pole with her entire body like someone who's riding the bus for the first time. The bottom fell out of my stomach.

I lowered myself to the ground and went to her. She stared at the ground, one hand over her mouth, swallowing repeatedly. "Are you okay?"

She shook her head.

Frank swore. "I never should have let her do the routine, not in her condition."

I chafed at the idea that a woman needed a man's permission to do her job. "Excuse me? Let her? Penny is a grown adult. She makes her own decisions."

"Maybe, but I'm the doctor here," he retorted. "One day without morning sickness doesn't mean she's at one hundred percent. I know better than anyone how dancers push them-selves too hard."

"Can we please argue over whose fault this is later?" Penny asked weakly. "I need to sit."

"Oh, no. I'm sorry, Pen." I helped her hobble to a folding chair in the front of the room. "We need to get you back to the cabin."

"She should go to the infirmary." Frank put his hands on his hips and glared at me.

"I'm *fine*," Penny said loudly. "Give me a few minutes, and I can get back to the room myself."

"Someone should walk with you," I insisted. "You're not yourself."

Penny's hands shot to her hips as she pulled herself as upright as she could from her position on the chair. "Then call Guillermo, because he's the only person besides Robbie who knows what's going on. You've got a lot of work to do. I can't cut into your practice anymore."

Frank glanced at his watch. "The infirmary is closer than your cabin."

Penny and I exchanged an amused look before I said, "Let me make the call."

I wanted to go with my friend, tuck her into bed, make sure she was okay. But I couldn't walk away from the little time we had to practice. With a sigh, I opened a panel on the wall and pulled out the shipboard phone.

After Penny left, we resumed the workout. The tension from our argument hung in the air, but we needed to keep going. I spoke woodenly, trying to keep my emotions from getting the best of me again. Every minute lost weighed heavily on my conscience. We had to get this right, and we didn't have much time.

If life were an '80s movie, our rehearsal felt like the inspirational training montage. Except the sight of me hitting the ground over and over and over wasn't terribly inspiring. I'd simplified the original routine since Frank didn't have much time to learn the moves. I cut some of the more difficult positions that Penny and I did, and I substituted some that required strength for poses that showcased flexibility. I was a good teacher, but I couldn't give Frank years of stretching in a few days. He hadn't kept up on his exercises, so despite being in good shape, he wouldn't be doing splits any time soon.

One move, however, needed to stay: our showstopper. I'd fought with Max to be allowed to do it, because he worried that it was too risqué. The prude. He wanted me to tone the whole thing down. Instead, I'd ramped it up a notch or two. As long as the audience loved it, he'd forgive me.

At the end of the original routine, Penny and I did a running leap onto the poles, grabbing them between the tops of our thighs while gripping with one hand. The other hand reached out in front of us, legs extended in back to give the illusion of flying.

"I'm no Superman," Frank said after I showed it to him for the dozenth time.

"You can hold the pose easily," I said. "It's the mount you're having trouble with. And that's all in your head."

"Really? It's all in my head that it's a bad idea to take a flying leap at a metal pole, castrating myself when my balls hit it at ten miles per hour. That's the hill you're willing to die on?"

I glared at him until he broke into a sheepish smile. "Okay, maybe we're running like two miles an hour."

"I suggest you avoid slamming your testicles into the pole," I said. "But just in case, there's a cooler full of ice in the corner."

"Thanks." He pulled himself to his feet. "Let's try it again."

We pushed off together. Step, step, step, jump. I gripped the pole easily, as I'd done a thousand times. Frank got one hand on the pole, but his legs flew forward past their mark. He got his other arm behind him, holding him aloft long enough to lower his legs gently. Then he groaned and smacked the pole with one hand.

I dismounted. "That's much better!"

"I missed."

"But you didn't dent the mat with your ass this time. It's progress."

He glared at me.

"Try it again."

Frank sighed. "What time are we done?"

My temper flared. It was on the tip of my tongue to tell him to walk away whenever he wanted, and I'd do the routine myself. At the moment, having a nauseated Penny writhe on the floor while I performed seemed slightly preferable to continuing this farce. But I needed him, and he knew it.

"Soon. We can come back to that move later. Let's climb up, pretend we got it, and do the suspended inverted vee."

"Fine."

Up the pole I scrambled, as easy as pie. Beside me, Frank did the same, his years of dance training showing. Once he got into position, he leaned over and reached a hand out to me. I gripped it, then gazed into his eyes.

"Ready?" I asked.

He nodded. I could see the exhaustion on his face, but also the determination. We'd get this, even if it took all week. For this move, he would hold me in the air while I gripped his hand and swung backwards, rotating my legs over my head and spreading them in a vee. We'd practiced several times. Frank's part required a lot of strength to hold me up, but his moves weren't terribly advanced. Most of the work was done by the person swinging on the bottom.

He tugged, and I let go of my pole.

Frank's arm dropped, as expected. I swung my legs toward him.

His fingers opened, and my hand slipped out of his grasp.

I landed on the mat with a loud thud. Tears stung the corner of my eyes, and a loud grunt escaped me. We used a four-inch thick mat for a reason, so I'd be fine, but the impact knocked the wind out of me.

Frank let out a sound of surprise, somewhere between a laugh and a scream.

My back stung, but my pride hurt more. We'd never be ready at this rate, and this week would be for nothing. With that thought, I lunged to my feet, suddenly on the offensive. "Are you trying to kill me? Do you think this is funny?"

He dismounted. "Yes, actually, I find this hilarious. I love making an ass of myself. This is way more fun than exploring the Cayman Islands. I love missing my entire vacation so I can bruise myself. I still can't do the Superman mount, I'm not clear on all the spins, I have no idea what I'm doing half the time, and part of me is still worried you're going to tell me at the last minute I have to learn a Fonzi."

His mispronunciation of "fonji" broke some of the tension inside me.

Frank hadn't finished his rant, though. "I'm doing all of this to save your ungrateful ass, and yeah, part of me thinks you deserved to be dropped on it."

While he spoke, I really looked at him. A full examination. Redness ringed his eyes. His shoulders drooped. We'd been at this for hours, turning breakfast into a distant memory. At the reminder of food, my stomach growled, filling the room with angry noise. Suddenly, I felt terrible. Frank wasn't used to the four hour practices anymore. He hadn't signed up for this. He just wanted to keep his sister company while she took the Sassy Singles cruise. I'd been working him to the bone since Day One, while making snotty comments about rich people. Desperation had turned me into a person I didn't like very much.

I waited for a long moment after he stopped talking. "You done?"

He nodded. "I'm sorry my hand slipped. But, yeah, I'm done."

"I'm sorry," I said. "You're absolutely right. All of it. Let's take a break. Come with me."

Scooping up my clothes, I dropped into a chair in the corner to remove my shoes. Perhaps he expected more of a tongue lashing, because Frank stared at me for a beat before grabbing his shirt off the ground.

I grabbed his hand and led him through the bowels of the ship, not caring for once if anyone saw us. On port days, about a third of the staff went ashore, and everyone else worked. No one stopped to look at me. Minutes later, we'd arrived at the ferries carrying guests from the *Aphrodite* to the mainland.

A moment after we sat, Frank nudged me. "Does that woman look familiar to you?"

Since every single person on the ferry was also on the ship, I theoretically could have encountered any of them. Still, I looked where he was pointing. To my surprise, she did look familiar. I'd seen her face plastered across at least two of the celebrity magazines my sister read.

"Oh, yeah. She's on that show. Legal something?"

"*Legal Lies*," Frank said. "It's a good show. Do you get a lot of famous people on the ship?"

I didn't want to admit that my knowledge of pop culture was about as extensive as my knowledge of astrophysics. He was making conversation to diffuse the tension lingering from our argument, so I needed to meet him halfway.

After a moment, I remembered something he might find interesting. "Some. A rock star shot a video on Monday. And there's a baseball player getting married onboard this week."

"Interesting," Frank said. "So where are we going?

"First, food," I said. "Tell me more about yourself. Pole partners need to trust each other, and it's hard to trust a stranger."

"You think I can hit that mount once I get to know you better?"

"It can't hurt."

I sent him on ahead with instructions to meet me at a café

about three blocks down while I chatted with some of the other entertainers. Ten minutes later, I followed.

After our second breakfast, we went back to the docks, but not where the cruise ship dropped us off. The benefit of visiting the same ports time and again was knowing people at all of them. Today, we went to visit a friend's studio. It wasn't open, but she'd long ago given me a key so I could drop by and work out when in town. In exchange, I checked on the place when she left the island.

Frank stopped dead on the sidewalk and looked at me. "Aqua-batics? What is this?"

"Underwater pole dancing."

"You're joking."

"Nope. Water is the best place to work these moves," I said. "When I'm weightless, it's easier to work on form."

"This is my penance for dropping you," he muttered, but he followed me toward the giant tank. "You're going to drown me and leave me here."

"Don't tempt me," I replied.

My outer clothes hit the ground. I climbed up the ladder on the side of the tank, then dove off the platform into the water without looking back. Opening my eyes, I swam to the pole and gripped it in a very basic climb: one of the first moves we'd practiced. Then I searched for Frank on the other side of the glass, in the observation area.

When I didn't see him, my heart sank. For a split second, I thought he'd abandoned me. Then the water parted, and seconds later, he reached my side. I spun around, twisting my body into the flag position I'd demonstrated the first day of class. Frank gripped the pole about a foot above my head and did the same.

I grinned up at him, and he shot me a thumbs up. Relief flooded me. On the way here, a voice in my head had insisted this was a terrible idea, but it seemed to be working. Releasing the pole, I kicked to the surface and motioned for Frank to follow me.

"This is amazing," he said when his head broke the surface.

I grinned at him, relieved. "I'm glad you think so. Let's go through the moves."

"I've got a better idea," he said. "Tag! You're it."

Pushing off the pole, he sliced through the water. I watched him go, admiring the graceful way he moved. Then with a laugh, I took a deep breath and dove down after him.

When we finished, I collapsed onto the floor, grateful for the crash mats left for stretching. Following an intense workout, the two inches of foam felt more luxurious than any bed I'd ever imagined. Not even the Queen of England could sleep as comfortably as I felt right then. When Frank stretched out beside me a moment later, I moved over to rest my head on his shoulder.

Within seconds, I'd drifted off to sleep in his arms.

CHAPTER NINE

That afternoon, Frank and his friends had signed up for a tour of the island. Even if I'd wanted to, I couldn't ask him to cancel. After an exhausting morning dancing in the water, he needed rest. He also needed to spend more time with his friends. Luckily, Frank said Lisa threw herself into the Sassy Singles events, despite being interested in Robbie, so she gave Frank a lot of space.

I did, however, insist that he meet me after dinner. Worried that he would back out if he knew what I'd planned, I gave him the address of a diner a couple of blocks from our destination. When he arrived, I took his hand and led him through a maze of back alleys. He squeezed for a second, so lightly I might have imagined it. Or maybe our morning strengthened the connection for both of us.

"I'm almost afraid to ask," Frank said as he trailed behind me, "but where are you taking me?"

"It's a surprise."

We continued in silence, Frank glancing nervously around after every couple of steps. I suspected only his sense of chivalry stopped him from leaving me in this part of town. Thankfully, he didn't know I'd taken self-defense training when I started working the clubs. One of the bouncers showed me a few tricks in exchange for watching his daughters on my nights off.

After a few minutes, I drew to a halt in front of a dark, dingy building. Potholes filled the parking lot.

"You've got to be kidding me," Frank said. "If you wanted a drink, there are half a dozen places closer to the ship. Places where we don't have to worry about getting gonorrhea."

"Check your privilege," I told him. "This place is fine. In fact, it's exactly what we need right now."

He flushed and looked at the ground. Part of me felt bad. He didn't ask to be born rich. At the same time, he didn't have to be a snob.

I pointed at a sign in the window. AMATEURS' NIGHT. CASH PRIZE.

He shook his head. "Oh, no. Tell me you're not thinking what I think you're thinking."

A wide-eyed, innocent grin was my only response.

"I'm not ready."

"You are, but that's beside the point. You need to practice before an audience."

"And you don't think the guys in there will boo me off the stage for not being a beautiful woman?"

"Unlikely, since it's a gay bar."

He chuckled. "You think of everything."

"I've learned to be pretty resourceful. Come on."

Inside, the club looked much nicer. Clean, brightly lit areas around the stages, with comfortable seats and tasteful artwork. Frank let out a low whistle. "Why don't they fix the outside?"

"Maybe they're looking to keep out the upper crust." I winked at him.

Before he could protest any more, I signed both of us up for the evening's competition. They didn't have a doubles category, so we would perform alone. There was really no need for me to do a set, but I put my name down first. I figured Frank would feel more comfortable watching me before taking the stage.

I didn't ask about the prize money, assuming it would be around twenty bucks. Chump change for Frank and less important than the practice to me. The competition wouldn't start for another half hour or so, so I ordered us each a rum and cola. While I generally discouraged poling drunk–and wouldn't teach students who showed up under the influence–one drink should help take the edge off.

Of course, I hadn't expected Frank to empty the glass in one gulp and immediately order another. I put my hand on his arm. He said, "Don't worry, the drinks are on me."

"It's not that," I said. "You need to keep your wits."

"There are five people on the list ahead of us," he said. "I'll make the next one last, I promise."

I met his eyes squarely. He held my gaze, breathing steadily. I wanted to tell him no, that he could only have one drink before we performed. But this was the first moment since we arrived that he didn't look petrified, about to bolt at the slightest provocation, so I didn't argue. But if he ordered a third, I'd tip the bartender NOT to bring it.

Slowly, as the clock inched toward eight o'clock, patrons filled the bar. The ship left the port at ten, so I prayed the show started on time. While a professional pole routine could last four or five minutes, it took a lot of stamina to go on for that long, so amateurs usually stopped after about two to two and a half. Our routine took three minutes, fifteen seconds.

Finally, our host appeared. An Asian drag queen strode onto the stage wearing six-inch platform Pleasers that made her seem ten feet tall.

"Good evening, y'all! I'm Tabby Rangoon. How's everyone doing tonight?" With a microphone in one hand, she grabbed the pole with the other and swung her legs wide, twirling in a circle. The audience hooted and hollered. Her skills didn't worry me, but Frank swallowed hard.

"Relax," I whispered. "The host isn't going to be performing. She's a professional drag queen, not an amateur."

"What about you?" he whispered back. "Are you allowed to perform?"

"Probably not." I shrugged. "We're here for you. I don't care about me. My eye is on a bigger prize at the moment."

He nodded, and we fell quiet as the first performer took the stage. Strains of "I Just Don't Know What to Do with Myself" filled the room. Over the years, this song appeared at so many amateur nights that I finally borrowed my bouncer friend's phone to google it and find out why. The routine presented on stage reminded me of a less-polished version of the old music video I'd found online. A lot of smiles and winks, no terribly difficult pole tricks. Competitor Number 1 presented no threat.

The second performer was much better, throwing in a few spins and tricks. I wouldn't be surprised to learn that she'd taken some lessons or worked in a club for a couple of weeks. Frank's eyes widened a bit as he watched, but he didn't need to worry. He could out-perform Number Two in his sleep.

Then the third performer took the stage. The first male so far, and he'd been practicing. He twirled around the pole as if it were an extension of himself, swiveling and climbing and flirting with the audience like he'd been born doing it. Beside me, Frank's face went pale. If his spine stiffened any more, he'd turn to wood.

"Relax," I whispered, although it hurt to realize we might not win the cash. No matter how many times I said it wasn't about the prize money, deep down, Poor Janey knew the truth. "You're here to practice, get comfortable on the pole in front of people. There will always be other talented performers, you know that."

He nodded and took a couple of deep breaths. "I always get a little tense before a show. I'll be fine. I just need a few minutes alone to collect myself."

"You couldn't have mentioned that earlier?"

"I'll be right back." Before I could say anything, he bolted toward the bathroom.

Once again, I wondered at the wisdom of all of this. Maybe I should've spent the week trying to come up with a singles routine that would wow Max as much as the doubles presentation Penny and I planned. Or maybe the two of us should have written a new routine she could do...while vomiting?

I shook my head at the thought. Impossible. We'd had no choice but to find a replacement, Frank truly was a gift horse, and I needed to stop looking him in the mouth.

Even though he had very nice lips. And soft hands. Muscles that went on for days. Muscles I absolutely, positively should not touch outside of the practice studio.

The third contestant finished to thunderous applause. I gave him a standing ovation, more than happy to recognize the work that went into putting on such a show. For the first time, as he walked around the stage taking bows, I realized that bar patrons were tipping him, both men and women. Cash littered the stage. Maybe I'd be able to make a few bucks even without taking home the grand prize. The thought cheered me a bit.

When the fourth performer took the stage, Frank still hadn't reappeared. I glanced between the bathroom door and the bar's front door uneasily, but even in this crowd, it would be tough for him to escape without me seeing him.

Contestant Number Four went on and off the stage practically before I could blink. He might have been good, but with only a trick or two, he didn't stand a chance. Good news for Frank.

A moment later, Tabby called my name. Head high, I sauntered onto the stage. A couple of people in the crowd must have recognized me, because I heard a whistle here, a hoot there. Better news. Hopefully my fans tipped well.

The music started. For this performance, I'd chosen "Girl on Fire," my go-to girl power song. I didn't want to use the song from our routine and have Frank follow me with the same tune a few seconds later. Instead of the routine we'd been practicing, I went through the motions I'd done at the Welcome show the first night. It didn't contain my best tricks, but I spun and swung and got the crowd on their feet, warming them up for Frank.

When I finished, the crowd landed on their feet, smiles from wall to wall. I walked around picking up bills, grinning widely. The money scattered around my feet more than covered the drinks I'd bought when we arrived.

My smile faltered only when I looked at the side of the stage and realized I didn't know where Frank went. He easily could have escaped while I pranced around the stage. Even if I'd taken my attention off the routine to notice, I wouldn't have been able to stop him.

A pulse fluttered frantically in my throat at the possibility. If Frank abandoned me for this show, I didn't know what I'd do. He couldn't do the Talent Show finale if he wasn't able to handle a drunken bar crowd. With a final bow, I jumped down the few steps to the ground, eager to find him. He didn't seem like the type to sneak out; Frank wasn't a coward. On the other hand, he also didn't seem the type to hide in the bathroom, and he'd been in there a while.

The announcer took the stage behind me. "Next up, our fifth and final performer. Mr....Baby Cakes? Does that say Mr. Baby Cakes?"

On the stage, the announcer called Frank a second time. I was torn between wanting to show my faith in him and stampeding the restroom to find out what was taking so long.

"Come on, Mr. Baby Cakes. Don't be shy!" The announcer said. "We're all friends here. Aren't we? Let's give him a bit of encouragement!"

Applause scattered around the room. Still no sign of Frank. I held my breath. The spotlight moved around the room, unsure where to stop.

Terrified, I covered my face with my hands.

"Last call for Mr. Baby Cakes! Come on, sweet cheeks. You can't be worse than my cousin Leonard."

The audience erupted into cheers. I didn't dare look, but then the opening strains of the music began. Peeking through my fingers, relief flooded through me when I saw Frank strutting to the pole. I let out a whoop of joy, and he found me in the audience.

The look he gave me thrilled me to the core. He might be a bit shy, but Frank was a professional, and at heart, he loved to perform. He should be fine.

On the stage, Frank began the routine, moving competently, if a bit stiff. When he finished his first spin, the crowd applauded, and he loosened up. With every cheer from the crowd, his confidence grew. I let out another whoop, and he rewarded me with a giant smile.

Then the moment of truth arrived. The big move, the one that always gave us so much trouble in practice. The one we argued about yesterday.

Clasping my hands over my mouth, I watched as Frank let go of the pole. He paced five steps toward the back wall, away from the audience, as planned. When he turned, his eyes sought mine. I dropped my hands, hoping to convey reassurance and serenity.

With a deep breath, Frank ran for the pole. Step, step, step.

He leapt in the air, beautifully, as he must've done a million times when he danced ballet. More than anything, I wished I'd gotten a chance to see him perform at his peak. It must have been glorious.

Frank flew across the stage, exactly as we practiced. Then he...landed on the other side of the pole, making no move to grip it with his hands or legs. Instead, he put his hands out in the gesture I recognized from the *Aphrodite's* video bar incessantly playing "Walk Like an Egyptian" on '80s night. I groaned.

My hands came back up to cover my face. We were doomed.

After that brief hiccup, Frank executed the rest of the routine flawlessly. If you didn't know what we'd practiced, you might not know he'd flubbed the steps. Well, if you didn't know and if you happened to think funny hand motions belonged in pole performances. At least it wasn't jazz hands.

The final two performers were passable, but not terrible exciting. Once they finished, Frank and I took the stage, lining up with the others to find out who won.

"Our winner will be decided by the audience," Tabby announced. I'd known this, which was one reason I didn't expect to win, but Frank looked surprised. "One of you is going home with five hundred dollars!"

"Don't worry," I whispered to him. "This was about building confidence, not about winning a prize."

"You have no idea how competitive I used to be," he whispered back. "That's a lot of money."

Tabby pointed at each of us in turn, while the audience clapped and cheered. The crowd went wild for contestant number three, who had done an excellent job. On my turn, I stepped forward and curtsied gracefully to a respectable response. Ah, well.

Then Frank was up. He walked to the front of the stage, as

the rest of us had done. But he didn't stop there. When he got to the front, he spun around on his toes, turned, and wiggled his admittedly fine butt at the audience. The audience roared, but Frank wasn't done yet.

He turned around again, ripped his shirt over his head, twirled it around, and launched it into the crowd. Then he leapt up and executed a perfect ballet jump before landing in a split on the stage.

The crowd exploded. Even I couldn't help clapping until my hands hurt. Competitive, huh? It appeared that, in some ways, the student surpassed the teacher.

Frank returned to his place in line, and the final two contestants tried to reprise his last minute dance, but it was too late.

"Well, that was certainly something," Tabby said. "Ladies, gentlemen, and persons of all genders, we have a very clear winner here. The pole performance was interesting, but that encore certainly took the, er, cake. Congratulations to Mr. Baby Cakes!"

A whoop of joy escaped me. I'd never been so excited about someone else's pole performance.

Turning to me, Frank threw his arms into the air. "Hell, yeah, baby! That was epic!"

I slapped his hands. "Well done, Baby Cakes!"

After Frank collected his prize, the two of us headed for the parking lot, still high on our success. We had about half an hour to make it back to the docks, plenty of time if we walked fast. We made it about ten steps before Frank stumbled in a pothole. I caught him and started to ask if he was okay, but he just shook his head, laughing.

"Mr. Baby Cakes, huh? Very funny."

I shrugged, trying to seem cool. "We couldn't use your real name. Seemed fitting, don't you think?"

"It's fine. Tonight was perfect."

He picked me up and spun me around. My head fell back, hair streaming out behind me, and I let out a sound of pure joy. The kind of real laugh we use as children but repress when we get older and more aware of ourselves. It felt like nailing a difficult move on your birthday while finding five bucks in the pocket of a coat not worn all summer.

My arms wrapped around his neck. After a moment, he slowed the spins and lowered me to the ground. Inch-by-inch, my entire body became very aware of Frank's. Even though I saw him every day, I tried not to dwell on his physical perfection. (I'm not saying I succeeded.) Our eyes met when my toes touched the ground. I started to unwrap my arms, but Frank's hands moved from my waist to my chin, cupping my face.

He kissed my forehead with an emphatic "mwah!" that made me laugh. Then he kissed each cheek, the contact sending lightning bolts down my spine. Before I knew what was happening, his lips met mine.

The crowd faded away as the fire that had been smoldering within me all this time ignited. This wasn't an excited, accidental kiss. My mouth opened beneath his, and our tongues met eagerly. I wanted to taste him, to touch every inch of him. By the time I pulled back, my heartbeat thundered in my ears.

"Are you okay?" he asked.

I nodded, one hand covering my mouth. "What about Nellie?"

He furrowed his brow. "You want to kiss Nellie?"

"No. Don't you?" He gave me a blank look. "I thought the two of you were dating."

A peal of laughter rang out in response. "No. Oh, no. Nellie and I are not dating."

"I'm glad you find that thought so funny. When Penny mentioned it a few days ago..."

He placed one finger across my lips. "Penny made a joke

about 'my little girlfriend.' I thought she was referring to the fact that I've known Nellie most of my life. Our parents are old friends. But we're not, and have never been, dating. The only person I've wanted to kiss all week is you."

My heart soared higher with each word. "I've been wanting to kiss you, too. Since the moment I saw you."

"I'm glad to hear it." He leaned in, but I took a step backward. "See, I like that you're unpredictable."

"We're in public. I got carried away, but we can't. Not here. Someone could see us."

"Right." He pulled out his phone. "I'll get a car."

"I don't think they have Uber here."

He chuckled, a sound that made me bristle slightly. "They have taxis."

Taxis cost a lot of money, even for short distances. To be honest, I couldn't even afford Uber. Sure, he'd just won five hundred bucks, but I didn't want to take his money. "It's a beautiful night. Let's walk back. There's no rush."

He looked like he wanted to argue, but maybe he sensed that I didn't want him to pay for me to get back to the ship. The phone went back into his pocket. "I wouldn't say there's no rush. If I don't get you to my cabin soon, I might explode."

A shiver went down my spine at his words. "Good thing it's not far, then."

CHAPTER TEN

We spent the night in Frank's cabin. The moment my skin touched those luxurious white sheets, I never wanted to get up, and not just because of the gorgeous man beside me. Alas, morning found me back in the pole studio immediately after breakfast and the first shower I'd ever seen that held more than one person. The shower in the cabin Penny and I shared barely fit me.

Personally, I'd have been happy to languish all morning in that amazing suite, exploring my connection with Frank. Unfortunately, I had a class to teach before the passengers headed for the shore. After, Penny planned to join us for costume fittings. Frank obviously couldn't wear her outfit, so we needed an alternative.

As a former ballet dancer, Frank was used to wearing extremely tight, form-fitting clothing. What he wasn't used to was wearing very little at all. When Penny showed up with the shorts she'd been sewing for him all week, he balked. "That's a swimsuit. No, a speedo. It's a banana hammock."

"That's what male pole dancers wear," she said. "Look at Janey's outfit."

Beside him, I held up my lacy white sports bra-type top and blue sequined hot pants. Both covered exactly the amount of flesh necessary to keep from being indecent. Frank's eyes went from the minuscule clothing to my body and back, so appreciatively I blushed.

"Trust me," I said. "Go put it on, and we'll run through the routine to make sure everything stays in place."

"I want you to know I'm doing this against my better judgment."

"And I completely appreciate that," I said. "You're the best."

"What are you doing, Janey?" Penny asked when Frank disappeared back into the locker room to change.

"It's fine. I'm fine." Quickly, I removed my warm-up clothes and slithered into the outfit, turning to model the ensemble for my friend.

"Are you? Because it looks like you're about to get fired."

"I'm being careful," I said. "And it doesn't matter. We'll never see each other again after he leaves the ship on Saturday morning."

She started to say something, but a sound from the locker room stopped her. She simply shook her head and made some adjustments to my clothes as Frank re-entered the room, holding a gym bag in front of his crotch.

"Come on," I said.

He stared at me for a long moment but finally dropped the bag. The shorts looked fantastic on him, leaving little to the imagination. Despite my better judgment, I allowed my eyes to feast on the flesh I'd so enjoyed touching only a few hours earlier.

Nervously, Frank tugged at the fabric, trying to get the shorts to cover more of his butt.

"Stop," I said. "You look great."

"Mmm-hmmm. Great," Penny said. "Look, I gotta go before Max comes looking for me. Janey, I'll talk to you later."

"Wait." Frank went to his bag and pulled out an envelope. "Before you go, I want you to have this."

"What is this, a tip? I haven't done anything for you," Penny said.

"It's the money I won last night. Five hundred dollars."

She gasped. Her incredulous expression must have been mirrored on my own face. He was just going to give her five hundred dollars, like it was nothing. I couldn't believe anyone would do something so nice for someone they barely knew. "You're joking, right?"

"I'm dead serious. I don't need the money. You're about to have a baby."

"I'm not taking charity," she said.

"It's not charity," he said. "I would never have been there if it weren't for you. I loved every second of it. Consider it a thank you."

She continued to protest, but I moved between them and took the envelope, pressing it into her hand. "Say 'thank you, Frank.' You need this, Pen, and we both know it."

"Thank you, Frank."

"You're welcome," he said. "Now go rest. And thank you, Janey."

We stood in silence for a moment after she left. "That was an incredible gesture."

"Yeah, well, I thought about giving you the money, but I figured you wouldn't take it."

"Don't give me too much credit," I said. He didn't know my dad was sick, though, and I really wouldn't take his money. Probably.

"Be sure to give yourself enough credit. Anyway, let's look at these costumes." Apparently, gratitude made him uncomfortable. Frank joined me beside the mirror, and I turned. In our matching outfits, we looked like a great team. "Perfect."

"Not too shabby, I guess," Frank said. "Shall we practice?"

I took his hand. "Let's do this."

After our second time through the routine, I found myself extremely grateful that I'd talked Max into investing in the good crash mats for the pole studio. He probably never envisioned the use Frank and I put them to, but until about twelve hours earlier, neither had I.

A week ago, I never would have begun to consider having sex in my studio with anyone, much less a passenger. Frank made me throw all caution to the wind. Now I understood what people meant when they said someone made them feel like a teenager again. The difference was, with my mom leaving and dad's illness, I never got a carefree childhood. Frank made me feel like a teenager for the first time.

"Tell me about your mom," Frank said as we recovered from our session. "You don't talk about her."

Talking about the woman who gave birth to me required me to think about her, something I resolved never to do unless absolutely necessary. She certainly never thought about me after she left.

"Painful memories?"

I swallowed. "Very few memories. My dad raised me and my sister alone."

"I'm sorry to hear that. Did she die?"

"Might as well have," I said. He flinched. "She never wanted kids, but somehow wound up with two. Resented the way her body changed and her career stalled after the two of us were born. When I was three, she called a baby-sitter, went out for groceries, and never came back. My sister remembers living with her, but I don't."

"That must have been rough."

"Yeah." Once I started talking about her, the words bottled up in my chest, all desperate to escape at once. "They divorced a couple of years later. Dad asked for sole custody, and she didn't even fight him. She did, however, take him back to court once a year, every year, to reduce her child support payments."

He gasped. "Seriously?"

I nodded, not wanting to explain that most people only looked out for themselves. A woman who would abandon her children didn't want to send them money each month, even when a court order said to.

"What about visitation?" Frank asked.

"Never exercised it, and Dad didn't want to force her to see us. I asked him about it a few years ago." My throat thickened at the memory. "He said that it didn't benefit me or Heather to sit there while Mom went to a salon and got her nails done, ignoring us. Or worse, called a baby-sitter."

"That's so awful," Frank said. "I'm sorry."

"Don't be. He's right. A terrible visit wouldn't have made me feel any better than all the skipped and cancelled visits. At least in the beginning, I could pretend she wanted to see me but something important kept her away."

"So that's it? She left, took your dad back to court a few times, and that's it?"

"Pretty much," I said. "At the last hearing when I was eight or nine, the judge cancelled her support and visits with us. Dad wasn't even there. He couldn't afford a lawyer, and he couldn't take the day off work."

"The support wasn't enough to make up for one day off? Or to help him get by while looking for a better job?"

I wanted to shake my head at his naiveté. To Dad, getting himself fired would be as alien a concept as flying to the moon. We needed his paychecks, lived month to month. "Not when she never paid," I said. "He couldn't risk it."

"Wow. That's a lot for a child to carry around."

"I didn't know, at the time," I said. "Dad protected us. Said she was sick, or taking care of her parents. Or she got a new job with a boss who wouldn't let her take time off to come see us. Maybe we accepted what he said at face value because we didn't want to know the truth."

"How did you find out?"

"When I was a teenager, Dad and I had a big fight. Something stupid, I don't even remember what. I told him I wanted to go live with my mother. It was the saddest I've ever seen him look, to this day. But even then, he never said anything bad about her. Called her up, tried to arrange a meeting. We still had a landline for emergencies, couldn't afford cell phones. I listened in." I paused, swallowing hard at the memory.

Leaning over, Frank took my hand in his, rubbing my palm with his thumb. The intimacy of the gesture soothed me. "It was bad, huh?"

"Horrible." I sniffled and rubbed my forehead with the back of my other hand. Frank waited patiently until I continued. "I heard everything. Dad *begged* her to meet with me, even to have lunch or coffee. A one-hour meeting. She refused to give me even sixty minutes out of her life when I was desperate to see her. He asked her to at least talk to me and explain that she didn't have room for me to live with her, and she wouldn't do it. After less than ten minutes, I burst into tears and slammed down the phone."

"Did you get in trouble for listening?"

I gazed off into the sea for a minute for answering, strangely calm. "No. Dad never even mentioned it. He had to know. When he came back into my room later, I asked him to take me for ice cream. We talked about school and boys and neither of us brought it up again."

"Where's your dad now?"

Part of me didn't want to tell him, didn't want any more sympathy. But partners needed to be open and honest with each other. "He's in assisted living. That's why I need this job. I send every spare cent to help with his care."

"Oh." The sound filled the room.

I didn't know what else to say, and maybe he didn't, either. The two of us sat in silence for several minutes, lost in our own thoughts.

"Tell me a story," I said suddenly. "You've heard about my sad life. Tell me about your happy one."

He opened his mouth, just as a loud clack shot through the studio. Someone unlocked the top bolt on the outer doors. Meaning they'd be here in a matter of seconds. I shot to my feet, yanking my shorts up and a bra over my head in record time. Suddenly I was grateful that pole required so little clothing.

Frank grabbed his discarded clothes off the mat, scooped up the underwear that somehow landed in a far corner, and scurried through the door leading to the locker room. Never had I seen a grown man move so fast.

By the time Max stood in front of me, I was very calmly buckling my shoes. If he noticed my flushed face or accelerated breathing, he attributed it to the strenuousness of my workout.

"Janey! I've been looking for you everywhere."

"Sorry. Just going over the routine for the Talent Show."

He looked around the room. "Alone?"

"Penny will be here later," I said.

"Okay. So listen, that's what I wanted to talk to you about."

"Really?" My ears perked up.

"Yeah. We're taking a chance on a pole fitness performance because this is a singles cruise, where the crowd is a bit younger and more open-minded."

What about the fact that my classes have been packed every day? I wanted to ask, but didn't. Pole was gaining in popularity, and not just among millennials. But Max didn't drop by to chat. If he wanted to talk about the performance, he had something on his mind. I motioned for him to continue.

"Make sure you bring your A-game," he said. "This is one risk that has to pay off."

"Oh, it'll pay off," I said. "I've been thinking of ways to sexy up the performance, put in some more daring moves. The routine we talked about seems a bit robotic in places. Even some more fun music might shake things up a bit."

"We're not looking to 'shake things up'. Your job is to show people the kind of things they can learn from you if they book a second cruise. The types of things their kids can learn. No one wants their kids to grow up to be a stripper."

The words lanced my heart, but I forced my tone to remain steady. "You think so? I mean, it seems like putting our best foot forward–"

"Look, you're welcome to do whatever you want for your part of the show," he said. "But your contract is up for renewal at the end of the month, and we're looking to staff the *Aphrodite* with team players, if you get my meaning."

He couldn't be more clear: I could play along. Do the boring end-of-cruise demonstration he mapped out for me and Penny and keep my job or be bold, entertaining, and unemployed. If only I had anywhere else to go, but I didn't. Even with the money I'd saved over the past couple of years, it wasn't enough.

Biting my tongue, I nodded. "I'm happy to do the routine we talked about. It's going to look great."

"Excellent! I'm glad you see things my way." He offered a thin smile that made me want to throw up on him. I held his gaze, not reacting, until he walked away.

As soon as the door shut behind him, I let out a sound of frustration that echoed through the room.

"Why did you do that?" Frank's voice came from behind me.

Caught up in my conversation with Max, I'd forgotten that he waited in the locker room.

"Sorry," I said. "He's so frustrating sometimes! I've got so many great ideas–"

"Not that," Frank said. "I get why you're frustrated. I want to scream at that guy, too. I mean, why did you let him talk to you like you're nothing?"

The question threw me off guard. I looked at him, thinking. Until that moment, nothing seemed off about Max's tone; it simply was the way things were. "Max always talks to me like that. A lot of people do, honestly."

"You should stand up to them! Come on, Janey, you're always talking about how unfair the world is. Maybe if you stood up for yourself, things would be better."

"If I stood up for myself? Are you serious? If I tell Max what I think about his stupid ideas, I'm out of a job."

"So you're out of a job. You can find someone to work for who treats you better. Treats you the way you deserve."

"Oh, really? You hiring?" I shot back. His words frustrated me to no end. What must it be like to be born rich, white, and male in America? When we met, I thought we saw the world differently, but sometimes we weren't even looking at the same world.

Frank let out a breath. "I'm sorry. I just meant...you deserve better. I wish I could help."

"You *are* helping," I reminded him. "And I know it sucks, but it is what it is. Max is the worst. We all know it. I need this job, so I deal with it."

"And you're going to let him tell you how to do your routine?"

A smile curved my lips. "Of course not. We're doing the routine my way. The crowd will love it so much, Max'll look like a fool if he fires me."

"Damn right. We'll show him."

CHAPTER ELEVEN

*M*ax's interruption left me irritated, so we decided to take a break and go get something to eat. The two of us meandered through the crowds on the Lido Deck, not talking. Part of me was still frustrated that, no matter how much time we spent together, Frank didn't get what it was like to be me. I couldn't throw my career away in favor of my principles.

All of a sudden, Frank's eyes widened. He grabbed my arm and yanked, dragging me behind a stack of unused deck chairs. Into the shadows.

Shaking my arm out of his grasp, I gaped at him. "What are you doing?"

At that moment, a voice reached my ears. High-pitched, snooty. I had no trouble visualizing the speaker. "Jake, are you sure you saw Frank? Why would he be in here when he said he planned to spend the day at the casino?"

The casino. Yet another difference between us. I couldn't imagine putting my hard-earned money into a machine and hoping more came out, but that's because I couldn't afford to lose.

A male voice responded, deep and gravelly. It was the first

time I'd heard Frank's friend speak, which suddenly seemed odd. "I swear, I saw him walking next to someone."

Frank's arm tightened on mine, holding me in place.

"Who would he be with? We're all here, and Nellie's meeting Max for lunch." Another female voice, this one unknown to me. Probably Jake's wife, whose name I couldn't remember. "Come on, it's too loud up here, and my feet hurt. I'm going up to the adults-only hot tub to relax."

"Fine, I'll look for him myself. I don't know why I have to do everything." Lisa again.

The other woman huffed, her voice already further away. "Jake?"

"Coming. Lisa, we'll see you there." His voice faded as he spoke, so I assumed they were walking away from us. Of course, they didn't know that, because for some reason, Frank and I were hiding.

I pushed him away. "What are you doing?"

"Shh!"

This was stupid. We had things to do, and we were allowed to walk around on the same deck. Instead of answering him, I turned to leave. Before I could move, Lisa appeared before us, her mouth opened in such a perfect "O" of surprise, it had to be an affectation. "Francis?"

Instantly, Frank dropped my arm and stepped away from me. "Hey, Lisa. What's going on?" His voice was three octaves higher than usual.

"Hi," I said, not liking the vibe this scene gave me.

"We've been looking everywhere for you." Lisa glanced toward me for half a second before her lip curled. "Why are you talking to this stripper? I hope you've got hand sanitizer."

Frank stammered. He looked back and forth between me and his sister, clearly at a loss for words. It would have been so easy to say the truth, or that we'd become friends, or even that he'd been taking dance lessons from me. But he said nothing.

I thought we'd formed a bond, especially after last night. As the silence stretched between us, the enormity of my mistake hit me. This was all wrong. I couldn't stand here and let Lisa disparage me while Frank stood in silence.

"We're not doing anything." I moved past Lisa, toward the railing and the open air. Suddenly, standing so close to Frank was stifling. "Nothing at all. After all, I'm just 'the help', right?"

"Janey, wait," he said. "It's not what you think."

But it was what I thought. The answer was as clear as the nose on his face. No further explanation needed.

"Is this what you were talking about?" I asked him. "Not letting people talk down to me? Standing up for myself to improve my situation. Why aren't you standing up for us?"

His face turned white. There was no point waiting for a reply. Without another word, I turned and ran. He'd never follow, not when the people who mattered might see.

Although I didn't specifically decide to go there, my feet carried me across the planks to my studio where I could expend my energy the best way I knew how: On the pole. Queueing up my special "angry chick rock" play list, I climbed to the ceiling, spread my arms, and screamed. It felt good, so I screamed again. The soundproofed walls shouldn't allow my rage to penetrate the walls of the spa next door, but I didn't care. I simply let myself go.

My legs swung open, and I plummeted toward the ground, snapping my thighs shut at the last second to avoid slamming into the ground. One of my favorite moves, and always a crowd pleaser. Then I dismounted, turning and placing my shoulder against the pole before rolling my body upwards. I went through the most difficult moves I knew, wearing myself out too much to think.

An hour later, my rage spent, Frank found me slumped against the wall in the shoe closet, sorting pairs for lack of anything better to do. "Hey."

I glared at him, then continued chucking shoes into one of two bins. He flinched as the first shoe whizzed by his hip. Each pair landed with a satisfying thud. I didn't ask what took him so long to come find me. Probably talking to his friends about how many cars to buy with their buckets of cash.

"I know you're mad at me. I deserve it."

Since that was the truth, I still didn't answer. Staring up at him from this position was putting a crick in my neck, so my stony gaze moved to the floor.

"Don't I get a chance to explain?"

"There's no need. I get it. You were looking for a good time, figured the former stripper would be perfect for a roll in the hay. If you'll excuse me, I need to practice."

He moved, allowing me to push past him. But when my shoulder brushed his chest, he gently touched my arm. "Please. It's not like that."

"Then how is it?"

"You scare me." His voice trembled. "I've dated a lot, but I've never met anyone like you. I think about you all the time. I know we come from different worlds, but I don't care."

"If that were true, you would've defended me to your sister."

"I'm sorry. I panicked, and my brain froze."

"When your first instinct is to make sure no one knows we know each other, that's a problem. One I don't have time for. I'm sorry. This was a big mistake."

"What about the performance?" He asked as I walked past

him, toward the poles. "You still need to blow everyone away, and there's no time to teach the routine to anyone else."

He was absolutely right, but in that moment, I didn't care. "I'll manage."

"Big words from someone who was desperate for my help a few days ago." He increased the pitch of his voice to sound more feminine. "'Help me, Baby Cakes, you're my only hope.'"

"I made a mistake." My voice shook, betraying my bravado for what it was. "I can do it on my own. Just like everything else in life. Relying on you was stupid."

He crossed the room in three strides, stopping and spinning around in front of me. "That's what I'm trying to tell you. You don't have to do anything alone. Not anymore. I'm sorry. I'll fix it."

"What are you going to do? Tell her that we're friends and maybe more? Or maybe even suggest that she shouldn't treat people badly because they happen to work in entertainment?"

"Absolutely." He paused, and my heart stopped. "Right after the finale."

"You mean once the cruise is over and you never have to see me again."

There it was. My words hung in the air like a slap in the face. The thing neither of us wanted to acknowledge. Once the ship docked back in Miami, we were done.

Frank sighed, running one hand through his hair. "I meant, after the performance. Lisa's been spending a lot of time with Robbie and Max and Nellie. I tell her about us, she'll tell them."

Nellie. There she was again. He'd said they weren't a couple, and yet she seemed to turn up a lot. "Why does it matter if Nellie knows about us?"

"I'm worried about *Max*."

"You didn't answer my question." To avoid his eyes, I climbed up the pole. Having something to focus on made it easier to contain the emotions roiling around inside me. "You said earlier that you and Nellie aren't a couple. Does it matter if she knows about us?"

"It's complicated."

"Enlighten me. I've got nothing but time."

"It doesn't matter if Nellie knows about us. Like I said, we're not a couple," he said. "But her parents think we are."

"What? Why?"

"Nellie's mom's family owns the cruise ship. Her father is a doctor," he said. "Growing up, Dr. Kellerman wanted Nellie to follow in his footsteps. In a way, she did: playing softball, going to Princeton like he did. But whereas he went on to medical school, Nellie is terrified at the sight of blood. She couldn't do it, got her MBA instead."

"What does that have to do with you?"

"Since Dr. Kellerman can't leave his medical practice to his daughter, he wants the next best thing: a son-in-law. He loves me, always has. He's part of the influences that sent me to medical school after my accident. He wants to make me his partner. He also wants me and Nellie to get married."

"So what, you're using her?" Just when I thought nothing in this situation could horrify me more, he told me that he was pretending to date an old friend to get her father's medical practice.

"No." Behind me, I heard him pacing in frustration. "Would you please look at me?"

Without a word, I released the pole and fell backward, bringing my eyes near his level.

"Thanks," he said. "I told the truth earlier. Nellie and I aren't getting married. We're not even dating. She has reasons for wanting her parents to think we're a couple. Our charade makes an old man happy. Until today, it never hurt anyone."

"Whatever," I said. "It's none of my business. It's fine."

"No, it's not fine." He approached the pole, earnestness written all over his face. "Because I met you. No one has ever made me feel this way. I don't want to let Nellie down, she's a good friend. But I can't imagine stepping off this ship on Saturday morning and walking away, never again meeting anyone who makes me feel like you do."

A tiny voice in my head whispered not to get my hopes up. "You're not just saying this?"

"Please trust me." He stepped forward, bringing his face inches from mine. "No one has ever consumed my thoughts the way you do. No one makes my body tingle at the thought of touching them. And no one has ever filled me with despair at the thought of never seeing them again."

With all my heart, I wanted to believe him. Life without risks might mean safety, but it was also boring. I didn't get into pole to be boring. I did it to fly. Frank made my heart soar.

We shouldn't be doing this. I'd thrown caution to the wind the past couple of days, even though I could get into a lot of trouble. The way he was looking at me made it difficult to care.

Reaching out, I gripped his hand. "I don't want us to end on Saturday morning, either."

We'd been in this position before. Frank the Mary Jane to my upside-down Spiderman. Unlike our first lesson, this time, no one was here to interrupt us. I couldn't bring myself to move away. My lips parted, and my breath came in pants that had nothing to do with the energy required to hold myself aloft.

All of the air left the room as we gazed at each other for an eternity. Refusing to break eye contact, I waited patiently. Finally, Frank cupped my face in his hands. Even though it was a simple touch, after the anticipation, I moaned with pleasure.

He moved his hands up and down my cheeks, and I closed my eyes, savoring the sensation. A moment later, his lips touched mine softly, as if seeking permission. I kissed him back, then opened my mouth with a soft sigh. My arms came around to bury themselves in his hair, no easy feat while hanging upside-down. We stayed that way, exploring each other, until my legs began to shake.

Frank pulled back, ending the kiss. "You okay?"

"Never better." I slid down the pole in a basic dismount, not trusting my muscles to get back upright. When I neared the floor, my arms went up and my head tucked, allowing me to roll down slowly. Then I pulled myself to my feet before turning to face him as if Frank were a beacon calling me to the shore. I needed to turn and walk away, end things now before my weakness for Frank swept me away in an undertow.

I shouldn't be doing this. Each time would make it harder to say good-bye at the end of the week. We were too different. I'd get fired. And yet, it didn't matter. I was floating in a sea of Frank, and I'd rather drown than swim for the shore. Only that moment mattered, the feel of his lips on mine. The touch of his skin on mine, the whisper of zippers opening and clothes hitting the floor.

CHAPTER TWELVE

Finally, the day arrived. After a grueling week of secret practices and extra stretching and squeezing dance moves into every second I wasn't teaching or working a show, we made it to Friday. I'd barely slept all week. I'd eaten only when my growling stomach reminded me of the dangers of skipping meals while dancing so much. Frank sucked up all my mental energy, as well as emotional.

In about fifteen hours, I would know if any of it was worth it. We just needed to get through the final performance. But first, my schedule contained back to back classes all morning, so Frank and I agreed to meet in the pole studio at seven to run through the routine again.

My alarm woke me at six-fifteen. I showered quickly and dressed in the dark, careful not to wake Penny. Even though she'd started feeling better, she needed all the sleep she could get. After I finished eating, I'd bring her food on my way up to the studio so she didn't have to leave the room earlier than absolutely necessary.

This early, the ship was peaceful. Staff milled around, most of us working twelve-to-eighteen hour days that started early, but not talking much until the sun rose. Early bird guests usually went to the Lido Deck or one of the restaurants for coffee and breakfast. Briefly, I wondered where Frank would be, but I shook the thought away. He also needed to eat before our practice, but I certainly couldn't waltz into the buffet and plop down into the chair beside him. The only thing more ludicrous would be to invite him to eat with me in the staff kitchen.

We had a long day ahead, so I loaded my plate with scrambled eggs, sausage, and hash browns before grabbing two slices of toast and a glass of orange juice. I slipped a banana and a granola bar into my bag to eat between classes and took a seat at one of the empty tables to mentally review the routine.

We could do this. When performed correctly, our routine was poetry in motion. Frank soared around the pole, reaching heights I barely dared to dream of. Turned out, his ballet training wasn't so far in the past, after all. Even now, imagining the way he looked while we practiced, my mouth watered. I couldn't wait to see him again. To touch him and taste him and... no. To dance. Everything else needed to wait, then we'd have all night together.

What an amazing night it would be. Now that I'd given in to temptation, it became more difficult to focus on the routine. But I had to. The performance mattered the most right now. After, we could explore each other until the ship docked. I refused to think about what happened once we disembarked in Florida.

The table shook, jerking me out of my reverie. To my surprise, Max stood on the other side, leaning heavily on the wood with both hands. He never ate in the staff kitchen, preferring to use his status to either get meals delivered to his room or visit the onboard restaurants.

"Good morning," I said. "Are you here to talk about tonight's show?"

"No," Max said. "Where were you last night around midnight?"

In truth, I'd been in Frank's cabin. Lying naked in his arms, looking out at the sea through the giant windows. It had been so peaceful, I hated having to leave him to sneak back in my room before the sun rose.

None of which I could tell my boss. Sure, this cruise was nearly over, but I had to think about my future with Oceanic.

I stalled. "Midnight? Why?"

"I have my reasons."

He stared at me, waiting for an answer. Someone must have told him about Frank. But if he only suspected, he would never get confirmation from me.

My brain cast about frantically for an acceptable answer. "In my cabin."

"Can anyone confirm that?"

Penny had been working the late show, and he knew it. At least two hundred people saw her pulling bingo numbers until one o'clock in the morning. My heart sank. The one person who could confirm my whereabouts was also the last person I could name. "No, I was alone."

"What were you doing?"

"Reading."

"Oh yeah?" Max scoffed at me. "You want to take me to your cabin and show me the book?"

No, I absolutely did not. For the first time in my life, I wished I had a cell phone that allowed me to read on it. Finally, I said, "There's a library on the ship."

"Okay, then. What were you reading?"

Now that was a stumper, sadly. Having never visited the on-ship library, I didn't have the first clue what books it housed. I tried to think of a book likely to be there that I had actually read, in case Max asked more questions. "Little Women."

"You were in your cabin reading Little Women?"

"Yes."

Either Max wasn't familiar with the book or guessed that I would be, because he dropped it. "We've got a report of an expensive ring going missing from a guest's bag on the deck. A witness says you were spotted nearby."

A choking sound escaped me. No way. "On deck at midnight? Near a bag? No way. Check the security cameras."

"There's only one camera covering that area, and it wasn't functioning. But I've got an eyewitness statement, and that's good enough for me."

"Then talk to them again. They've gotten me confused with someone else. Max, I'm not a thief."

"Didn't you grow up poor?"

The question sickened me. My spine straightened as I sneered at him. "Yes. Growing up poor taught me more respect for other people's belongings than spoiled rich kids like you ever have."

His face twisted into a grimace as he stared at me for what felt like forever. My heartbeat eventually slowed, but he didn't believe me. He knew I was lying, albeit not for the reasons he thought. He just couldn't prove it.

When he found out the truth, I was a goner. I couldn't prove I hadn't stolen anything. They didn't need to prove I did, not on a Panama-registered cruise ship where U.S. labor laws didn't apply. The terms of my employment could change at any time without notice.

I should resign. Tell him I'd leave the company at the end of the cruise, and let the investigation drop. But I couldn't stand the thought of people thinking I was a thief, when my only crime was losing my heart.

Instead, I leveled my shoulders and stared him down,

summoning every ounce of confidence I preached about in my classes. "Is that all you wanted to ask me?"

"No," he said. "What is your relationship with a passenger named Francis Hanson?"

His question sucked all of the air out of the room. Max wasn't investigating a theft at all. I opted for a partial truth. "I ran into him, literally, on Sunday before boarding. My ankle got twisted in the fall. He's a doctor, so he stopped by the studio to see if I was okay. He also took a beginner's pole class."

"That's it?" Max stared at me as a pulse fluttered frantically in my throat. I wondered if he could see it. "There's nothing else you want to tell me?"

At least that was an easy question. I absolutely didn't want to tell him anything else. "No."

"Entertainment staff are forbidden from consorting with cruise guests." He met my gaze and held it. This was it. He knew. He probably didn't know why, almost certainly didn't know about Penny's involvement. I needed to keep it that way.

Time to accept my punishment, if it meant keeping my friend's secret safe. "Okay."

"Is that all you have to say for yourself?"

Groveling wasn't my style. Neither was apologizing for following my heart. Pressing my lips into a thin line, I nodded.

"Well, okay then." Max stood, brushing his hands off as if the staff table might hold a host of germs. "You're fired. You've got one hour to gather your belongings. If you leave quietly, we'll still give you half of this week's bonus."

I couldn't believe my ears. I'd expected to be fired, but not removed from the ship. They couldn't let me hang out for the rest of the day, then disembark at dawn? "Leave quietly? Max, we're in the middle of the ocean. Where am I supposed to go?"

"We're not that far from land. Meet me in an hour in front of your cabin."

My cabin sat in the middle of the ship. For a horrifying second, I wondered if Max planned to put me in a lifeboat, then set me adrift. That would be horrible publicity, though, once someone posted pictures on the internet.

"We'll take you to shore," he said, as if reading my mind. "And Janey? One hour. Don't make me come find you."

Frozen in place, I watched him go. He wouldn't let me stay, even if I begged. Making a scene wouldn't solve anything. All I could do was go back to my cabin to gather my belongings.

But first, I needed to find Frank and say good-bye.

It didn't take long to locate my partner eating breakfast in the dining room with his friends. The four of them sat at a private table near the window, one of the nicer spots usually reserved for VIPs. Of course, Frank was a VIP, and I should never have let myself forget it.

"Excuse me," I said, approaching the table as formally as I could manage. "But may I speak with you privately for a moment?"

"Sure," he said. "Everyone, this is Janey. We've been spending a lot of time together during the cruise, which is why you haven't seen me around much."

Jake looked from me to Frank and watched as the tips of his ears grew red. "What, you taking dance lessons again, Frank?"

He stood abruptly, so fast the chair fell over backwards. "As a matter of fact, I am. Janey has been teaching me pole dancing. It's even more beautiful than ballet in some ways. I didn't tell you because part of me was ashamed, but that's ridiculous. The sport is a lot of fun, and it's incredibly difficult. You need both inner and outer strength to do it."

Lisa snorted. "Sport? Come on, Frank. You don't have to

drink the Kool-Aid to get into her pants."

Her words made me want to spit nails, but there was no time. As it turned out, no need. Frank turned on his sister. "Yes, sport. Pole is much harder than anything you've ever done, and it requires ten times the discipline. Something you'd know if you'd paid attention in class."

Lisa sputtered in response, but I ignored her. My heart swelled at the way he stood up for me. Too bad it was too late. I grabbed Frank's hand. "I'm sorry, but we need to talk."

"No problem." He dropped his napkin on the table and followed me out of the room.

I led him out a side door of the dining room that gave guests access to the restrooms. The hallway continued around the back of the ship to the auditorium, and private doors opened into dressing rooms. After looking up and down the hall, I used my employee ID to open one of those doors. Thankfully, Max hadn't deactivated it yet.

As soon as the door closed behind us, I whirled to face Frank. "Out there... your friends. You didn't have to–."

"Yes, I did." He held out his arms, and I sank into them. His lips found mine, and for a moment, it felt like everything was going to be okay. "I should've introduced you to them as soon as I started having feelings for you. I'm not ashamed of our rela-tionship, and I'm a jerk for making you think I was."

"Thank you." I buried my face in his shoulder, not wanting to have to tell him what happened. Someone like Frank never got fired from anything in his entire life. One hand stroked my hair as he murmured into my ear. The words didn't matter; the tone calmed me. Finally, I pulled back and met his gaze. "That's not why I'm here, though. This isn't about your friends."

"What happened? Is Penny okay?"

I shook my head. "No. I mean, yes, she's fine. It's..."

"It's okay, Janey. You can tell me anything."

"I have to go. Max fired me."

Confusion filled his eyes. "What are you talking about? I told them you weren't the one who stole the ring."

The words slapped me across the face. "Hold on. What?"

He ran one hand through his hair. "Lisa reported the theft of some of her jewelry last night and claimed she saw you on the deck of the ship. Turns out, she figured out why she kept seeing us together, and she got pissed."

Suddenly, everything clicked into place. This wasn't about any theft. If the ring even existed, Lisa must have hidden it. She didn't think I was good enough to be with her brother. To make up a crime, she must hate the idea of him consorting with "the help." Especially when Frank had a much more appropriate option in the form of Nellie.

"What kind of person accuses someone of committing a crime because they don't like them? Theft charges could stop me from getting another job, especially on a cruise ship."

"You'll be fine," Frank said. "There are plenty of jobs out there."

A sound escaped me, halfway between a laugh and a sob. Never had our differences stood out so starkly. "Can I please come live in your world? Because where I'm from, good-paying jobs aren't a dime a dozen and you don't file false police reports because someone hurt your feelings. In my reality, getting fired could mean not eating for a week and when someone accuses you of a crime, jail is a real possibility."

"I'm sorry," he said. "None of this is fair to you. I read Lisa the riot act, I insisted that she tell Max she lied, and I told him that I knew with one hundred percent certainty that you didn't do it."

A lump grew in my throat as I realized what happened. "You told Max the truth? To protect me."

"Yeah, I did. I let him know that you couldn't have been on

the deck at midnight because you were with me."

"Wow." Words left me entirely. I couldn't tell this wonderful man that his act resulted in the very thing he wanted to avoid. "I can't believe you did that. Thank you."

"So what's....?" Realization dawned across his features. "They fired you because of me."

I sniffled, struggling to maintain my composure. "'Entertainers are not permitted to consort with the guests.' I've got an hour to pack my stuff. Well, about fifty minutes now."

"I'm so sorry. This is all my fault."

"No, it's mine. I knew the rules, I broke them," I said. "And every second with you was worth it. I had the time of my life. I'm not sorry for what happened."

"Neither am I." His voice trembled, and he took a deep breath. "Let me talk to Max. Maybe I can get your job back."

Maybe in fantasy land. I didn't say it, because he meant well. But the fact that Frank was so used to getting whatever he wanted illustrated our differences perfectly. His world was champagne and caviar and talking your way out of any situation. My world was getting kicked while you were down.

We would never work. We'd never discussed having a future off this ship, because we both knew it couldn't happen. He wouldn't find me again after the cruise ended. I didn't want false promises.

There was nothing left to say, so I needed to go. Reaching up, I buried my fingers in his hair and pulled his lips down for one final kiss. I put every ounce of longing and tenderness into it. We'd go our separate ways, but I wanted him to remember this moment, what could have been ours in another life.

When I finally let go, tears mingled on both our faces. I didn't even know who shed them. Frank opened his mouth to say something, but I put my finger over his lips. Nothing he could say would make this moment sweeter.

CHAPTER THIRTEEN

*E*ven though I was ready when Max arrived at my cabin, it apparently took time to remove a fired employee from a cruise ship. They marched me to the personnel office to fill out forms, then Max got called away to deal with a crisis. Maybe he was just letting me stew because he could, but I waited in his office forever. By the time he returned, guests lined up outside the restaurants for early dinner. The final Talent Show would start in a couple of hours, but I wouldn't be taking part.

Finally, a speedboat arrived to carry me to the mainland. By the end of the cruise, we weren't far from our final destination in Miami, so that's where they took me. A minor consolation, since at least I wasn't getting dumped alone in a foreign country. I sat on the edge of my seat, staring at the *Aphrodite* as my boat sped away, imagining Frank on the deck, looking for me. Just in case, I didn't move, standing ramrod straight with the wind in my face.

Finally, the ship disappeared from view, and I fell to my knees, dissolving into tears. Now that I wasn't doing the show, Penny wouldn't get her bonus. If Max found out she was pregnant and couldn't dance, she might miss out on future work, too.

She couldn't afford to lose that money. What a mess. I'd ruined everything.

The only thing more miserable than being fired, losing my residence, and disappointing my friend was the realization that most likely, Nellie spent that very moment consoling Frank. Reminding him that they "belonged together" because they were lucky enough to be born rich. He's said they were just friends, but friendship often turned into more. They'd gone to the same schools, knew the same people. The differences between us were as vast as the ocean quickly creating more physical distance.

Maybe it was better this way. After all, the way Frank viewed the world fundamentally differed from mine. He might as well be from Mars, with his thousand-dollar phone, expensive degrees, and family-owned vacation home. I mean, seriously? He owned a house no one lived in. It just sat there, costing money in taxes and electricity and lawn maintenance and that didn't seem weird to him. Meanwhile, I couldn't fathom what it would be like to own one house, let alone two.

By the time we arrived at the docks, the sun was setting. I gazed out at the water, wondering how long it would be before the *Aphrodite* appeared on the horizon. Too long to stand here waiting, and what good would it do? Frank and I said our good-byes. We were done.

A cool breeze brought goose pimples to my flesh, jarring me out of my spiral of misery. I didn't know what to do, where to go, but I couldn't stand on here all night. Everything I possessed in the world lay at my feet in a couple of battered old duffle bags. I didn't have a smart phone, preferring to use prepaid devices when I landed back in the U.S. Usually I bought them on board before disembarking, but between saying good-bye to Frank and packing, it hadn't occurred to me. My best bet was to head for my sister's place. I may not have a job or love, but I'd have family and a roof over my head.

It was a start. With grim determination, I gripped the handles of my bags and started walking toward the road that would take me to the nearest bus stop.

Before I made it to the end of the pier, someone called my name. Turning, I saw Nellie standing about twenty feet away. My duffels crashed onto the deck. I blinked and rubbed my eyes, but the image remained. Of course, if my subconscious conjured up a vision of Nellie, she probably wouldn't be wearing the exact outfit I'd seen on the mannequin of the most expensive boutique on the *Aphrodite.*

"Janey, stop," she said. "I need to talk to you."

"Why? How are you even here? Didn't I just see you on the cruise ship?"

"A friend picked me up on their boat and brought me here. It's pretty fast."

Of course her friends owned boats. Nellie really was perfect for Frank in every way. They should buy a golf course and have a dozen children and live happily ever after. My stomach churned at the thought. I struggled to keep my voice even. "That's nice. What are you doing here?"

"I came to get you."

"And take me.... to jail? Sleeping with a passenger isn't a crime," I said. "Even if he's your fake boyfriend."

"He's in love with you."

My mouth fell open. If I hadn't already dropped my bag when I saw her, I'd have lost it at that point. "What are you talking about?"

"I've known Frank for years," she said. "My parents have been pushing us together since he started medical school. I totally get why. He's brilliant, charming, good-looking–"

"I don't need a catalogue of his good points. We can't be

together." My heart ached at the words, but if she'd come to help me, she needed to hear the truth. "We're from different worlds. It's only been a week. He'll move on. He belongs with someone like you."

"He belongs with the person who makes him happy." She took a deep breath before continuing. "I've always liked Frank. We get along great. But we're never going to be a couple."

"You looked pretty cozy on the ship," I said.

"It's an act," she said. "He pretends to be my boyfriend when my parents or their friends are around. It's easier than telling them the truth. But it's gotten out of hand. It's time to end the charade. We never meant to hurt anyone."

"Why now?"

"The fact that he told you the truth speaks volumes. Even Lisa thinks we're a couple." She paused to let the enormity of that sink in. "Frank and I never talked about what would happen if one of us fell for someone."

I wanted to believe her, but I couldn't wrap my head around what she was saying. I'd seen the two of them together. Witnessed the genuine affection on their faces. Could he be that good an actor? But if he wasn't, why would Nellie be here? Her story matched Frank's.

"We're too different. The two of you are a perfect couple. You should try dating for real."

She smiled at me. "Maybe we would, if Frank were a woman."

Realization dawned. That's why she needed to put on a show for her parents. Why she was so certain that she and Frank would never fall in love. It all made sense. "Oh. Well, thank you for telling me."

"You're welcome," she said. "Now, let's get back to the ship."

"You know Max fired me, right?" I assumed that being the owner's daughter didn't give Nellie any ability to override an assistant cruise director on staffing decisions. She worked in marketing or something, I thought.

"Yes, I do," she said. "And I'm very sorry, but I can't get your job back."

A twinge of disappointment hit me, but I hadn't allowed myself to truly expect anything better. I gripped the handle of my suitcase and straightened up to my full height. At least I could walk away with my head held high. "Well, thanks for the talk."

"But I am allowed to have guests."

Those words stopped me in my tracks. "What do you mean?"

"I've already talked to Penny. She's going to be at the show, waiting for my signal. The stage poles are ready to go."

"Why are you doing this?"

"Frank's miserable. He can't stand the thought of never seeing you again."

My lips twitched. "Gee, I don't have any idea what that's like."

"See? The two of you are perfect together."

"But–"

"Don't you dare tell me one more time that it can't work. Are you in love with him?"

Although there was no reason in the world for me to expose my heart to this woman, I answered immediately. A week ago, I'd have said you couldn't love someone you'd only known a week, but I'd have been wrong. "Yes."

"And he loves you. He wants to be with you, and not just until the cruise ends. Let's go get him."

"Did he send you to get me?"

"No," she said. "He has no idea I'm here. I thought it would be better, in case I couldn't find you. I didn't want to give him false hope."

Her words made my heart soar. She really did care about

helping us work things out. If she was right, Frank wanted to be with me. Maybe things would be okay after all.

"Well, then, let's go give him the shock of his life."

She pointed to a small boat in a slip about twenty yards away. "After you. We don't have much time."

CHAPTER FOURTEEN

I followed Nellie to a small boat that looked oddly familiar. While I once would've sworn that Nellie and I couldn't possibly have any overlap in our social circles, I knew the woman standing by the railing, waiting to welcome us aboard.

"Janey! Long time, girlfriend."

"Kelli-Ann! What are you doing here?"

"You two know each other?" Nellie asked, looking back and forth.

"Oh, yeah," Kelli-Ann said. "Janey's moves gave me the confidence I needed to kick my ex to the curb. I've never been happier."

"Those were your moves," I said. "I just gave you a few pointers."

"Whatever." She turned and gazed out over the horizon. "Shouldn't you be on that big-ass hotel where I found Nellie?"

"Janey's the one I brought you here to pick up," Nellie said. "Can you get us back to the *Aphrodite* in the next half hour?"

"Does a fish piss in the ocean?"

I didn't know the answer to that, but luckily, she wasn't

waiting for a response. Again, I wondered how she and Nellie knew each other.

"Of course I can! For one thing, the ship is headed to Miami, so it's moving toward us. We should catch it real quick. Come aboard." Kelli-Ann looked at my feet and held up one hand. "But first, take off those shoes."

Surprised, I glanced down at my feet. So much had happened in the past few hours, I didn't realize I still wore my five-inch purple glittery Pleasers. They made me smile, which is exactly why I put them on after Max fired me. "I've got other shoes in my bag."

"Change first, then join me on the deck. We'll head out as soon as you're ready."

Five minutes later, Nellie and I sped toward the slowly-increasing dot that represented the *Aphrodite* with Kelli-Ann behind the wheel. The clock on the wall confirmed that the Talent Show had already started, but I had enough time to perform the final number when I arrived. As long as Kelli-Ann got us there in half an hour as promised, that left me just enough time to get to the auditorium. It would be tight, but doable.

My foot tapped the deck as if I could move the vessel faster with the force of my impatience. To release some of my pent-up energy, I bounced up and down, stretching and warming up in case by some miracle we made it in time.

"I want you to know, I'm going to talk to my mother," Nellie said. "The way Oceanic treats employees is just wrong."

"Thanks for the gesture, but the cruise lines all do it. It's why they're registered in Panama in the first place. To avoid U.S. law."

"That doesn't make it right," she said.

I shrugged. She was being nice, and I appreciated it, but I also didn't expect anything to change. And now that I'd been fired, I'd never know.

"You don't believe me."

"It doesn't matter what I believe. If you think it's the right thing to do, do it. Not for me or Penny, but for everyone."

"You're right," she said. "I've got a seat on the board now. I'm going to make them listen."

"Well, I appreciate it, even though it's too late for me."

"Maybe not. Never say never."

I smiled at her. What I wouldn't give for some of that optimism. Time to change the subject. "How do you plan to get back on the ship?Somehow, I doubt they're going to stop for you."

"Well, they might stop for Nellie," Kelli-Ann said. "She's kind of a big deal."

She flushed. "They might stop, but that would take away our element of surprise."

"Good point," I said. "What happens when they see us coming?"

Nellie shrugged. "The Captain knows I got picked up. It's... not the first time I've snuck away for a few hours."

Her words gave me a new admiration for someone I once thought of as an uptight, spoiled rich girl. Nellie's life wasn't all perfection and roses. Having money didn't solve everything after all. It just gave you different options. I smiled at her. "You're not as boring as I thought."

"That's a relief," she said.

"So what's the plan?" Kelli-Ann asked. "The water's lower than when I picked you up."

"This close to shore, the ship is actually moving very slowly." Nellie pointed at a spot on one of the upper decks. "There's a hole in the railing."

"And you're going to what? Fly up there?"

It only took a moment to figure out the answer. No one could be better suited to break onto a cruise ship than me. "Don't be ridiculous. I'm going to climb."

"You're going to scale the outside of an eighteen-story cruise ship in high winds and hope you don't plummet to your death?"

"That's the plan." I gave her a wide smile.

"But the open deck is on the ninth level," Nellie chimed in. "So we only have to climb half of it."

I turned to her. "We?"

"Of course, I'm going with you. I want to see how this plays out."

With a skeptical look, I took in her entire outfit from head to toe. I didn't know much about clothes, but everyone knew Prada didn't come cheap.

Nellie rolled her eyes at me. "So I get a little wrinkled. We have irons. Besides, I've done this before, and I'm not wearing stripper shoes."

She never failed to surprise me. "Then I guess we'll climb together."

"I hope this guy is worth it," Kelli-Ann said.

"Oh, he is," I replied.

Kelli-Ann's skeptical look faded when we pulled close enough to the cruise liner for her to see the ladder on the outside. It was intended for maintenance and emergency use, but if getting Frank back wasn't an emergency, I didn't know what was.

"What about your bags?" Nellie asked. "Should I throw them up to you?"

My bags presented a problem I hadn't considered. As much as my new friend had surprised me in the past few hours, I wasn't prepared to test the accuracy of her throwing arm. "I can sling them across my back. They're not heavy."

Kelli-Ann shook her head. "I should've asked you to sign a waiver before agreeing to any of this."

After more than a decade of pole training, climbing a ladder was as easy as, well, climbing a ladder. Even the bags on my back didn't slow me down, since I'd trained wearing weights many times. Besides, I couldn't perform without my shoes.

With one last glance above, I turned back to hug Kelli-Ann. "Thank you so much."

"I want an update. And if you get married, you better invite me to the wedding."

Although I wasn't remotely thinking that far ahead, I nodded. "You got it."

"Now, go. You've got ten minutes."

Swallowing, I turned to the ladder and looked up. Ten minutes, several dozen rungs? No sweat. Probably. There was no time to worry about the math. All I could do was grip the nearest rung, place my feet on the ladder, and head upward. It would be harder once I got away from the minimal wind protection offered by Kelli-Ann's small ship.

Slow and steady. Up and up I climbed, trying not to think about the distance to the water below, the amount of time remaining before the show ended, or the fact that Frank might still turn me down once I arrived.

Below me, I heard Nellie breathing hard. A glance down showed her probably half a deck further down.

"Don't worry about me!" she called. "Go!"

I hesitated. None of this would be possible without Nellie's help. If I abandoned her and she fell, I'd never forgive myself.

She lunged upward, catching a second wind. "If you miss this chance because you're waiting for me, I swear I'll marry Frank purely to spite you."

A huge belly laugh escaped me, dispelling some of the tension. It felt good, but I didn't have time to relax. Instead, I turned back around and continued climbing.

Finally, I got to the opening and heaved myself onto the deck. My legs shook from the effort expended, so I allowed myself thirty seconds to sit and catch my breath before moving on. I didn't have much time, but I needed it. Below me, Nellie climbed on.

Virtually everyone on the ship was already at the show. The plus side was, no one saw me and Nellie scale the side of the ship. Unfortunately, it took longer to climb than expected, and I might be too late.

My bag thudded to the deck. I'd move faster without it, and Nellie could bring it. But more importantly, I needed what was inside. With a quick glance up and down the dock to make sure no one was watching, I stepped behind a staircase leading to the upper deck and changed into my costume.

Nellie pulled herself over the top rung as I finished. "You look awesome."

"Thanks."

"Now go. I'll bring your bags."

I didn't dare run on the wet deck. Instead, I gripped my shoes with one sweaty hand and set off, walking as fast as safety allowed. I didn't slow until I reached the auditorium doors.

At some point, Nellie fell behind again. She'd hopefully make it before the performance ended, but she'd made it clear not to wait for her.

From the other side of the doors, the faint strains of what had to be the final song reached my ears. Some corny feel-good song I wasn't familiar with but knew they'd planned to sing before the pole doubles routine. Max apparently hadn't come up with a replacement act.

Balancing on one foot, I buckled one shoe into place, then the other. Immediately, my confidence returned. Now I was in my element. A quick glance revealed that my costume was in place, unmoved by the race across the ship. I raked my fingers through my hair, catching the loose tendrils before scraping it back into a low bun. Then I threw my shoulders back, lifted my head high, and shoved the double doors with all my might.

They creaked open, moving slowly along the carpet. They didn't crash against the walls the way I envisioned.

On stage, the song continued. No one heard my entrance. No one noticed me. Well, that was about to change.

I strode down the main aisle in my five-inch heels, bra top, and booty shorts. When I got to the stage, I didn't turn to walk up the stairs. Instead, I placed my hands on the wood, pressed down, and hopped up. The singers trailed off, looking at me uncertainly. Whispers filled the room. Twisting on my toes, I turned to face the audience before rising to my feet. Then I strode to the center of the stage and took the microphone from a stunned Max.

He didn't resist. I could have pushed him over with a feather.

Into the microphone, I said, "Excuse me, ladies and gentleman. I'm Janey, former entertainer and dance instructor here on the Oceanic *Aphrodite*. I was supposed to end this show with a performance. This morning, they tried to tell me not to do it, that I needed to leave. But I came back. I want to show you all what I can do, and I want you to meet the performer I've been lucky enough to work with this week. I've always been proud of what I can do on my own, as a teacher, a dancer, a person. But now, I've learned to allow myself to accept help from someone else. More importantly, I've learned how to love.

"I'd like to introduce you to Dr. Frank Hanson."

The spotlights spun around the audience, highlighting Nellie near the doors for a second before settling on Frank. He sat at the end of a row with Lisa and his friends, beaming up at me. With a confused look on his face, he rose to his feet. Penny started clapping, then Nellie, and the crowd soon joined in.

I beckoned, and Frank walked toward the stage. Behind me, Penny and a couple of stage hands wheeled two performance poles out, locking them into the floor so the poles could spin but not move around the stage. When my partner reached the top of the stairs, I held one hand out to him.

Eyes never leaving mine, he moved toward me, taking my hand and dropping on one knee to kiss it. Then he stood up and kissed me, in front of everyone.

Cher had been right, apparently. It *was* in his kiss. The moment his lips touched mine, all my doubts fell away. We were going to do this. Not just the performance, everything. As long as we both cared enough to try, we'd work it out.

The cheers of the crowd surrounded us, then grew louder.

"I'm so glad you came back," he said when we parted.

"I couldn't stay away from you." Then I pushed him toward the pole. "Now, let's dance."

Frank wore khakis and a short-sleeved blue button down shirt to watch the show. That would never do for the performance. Eyes never leaving mine, he stepped out of one shoe, then the other. With a whisper, his pants hit the floor, revealing a tiny pair of navy shorts.

"You wore your costume?" I asked in disbelief.

"I never gave up on you," he said, shedding his shirt.

The music started as soon as we took our positions. Thanks, Penny. We moved to the beat as one, twirling, climbing, flipping, spinning. Pride filled me as I watched Frank out of the corner of my eye. No one would ever know he'd only had a week to learn to pole.

This was where I belonged. Nothing beat this feeling, like I could accomplish literally anything. My beaming face lit up the sky. I wanted to bottle this feeling, hold onto it forever.

When we got to the move that had given Frank so much trouble all week, the music slowed. My heart pounded in my ears, blocking out everything else. He could nail the move, absolutely. I had one hundred percent faith in him. But he needed faith in himself, or he might miss the pole and go flying off the stage into the audience. Or chicken out, like at Amateur Night.

I caught his gaze and gave him the smallest nod of encouragement. He met my look with sheer determination. Together, we walked away from our poles, toward the back wall. As one, we turned. Then, at the same moment, we burst into a run toward the poles, toward the front of the stage. Toward the audience. Step, step, step. We pushed off from the ground at the same moment. I flipped effortlessly, gripping the pole with my right hand and locking my thighs around the cool metal. For a split second, I couldn't look at Frank or see what he was doing, but I had total faith in him.

The audience gasped, then burst into applause. Twisting my body, I spun the pole to face Frank, one arm outstretched in the superhero pose.

On the other side, he mirrored me exactly. We'd done it!

I couldn't help it. A joyful peal of laughter escaped me. Then, as the music changed, I flipped myself over and climbed. To my left, Frank did the same. After we'd repositioned ourselves, we went back into the dual superhero poses. This time, I took Frank's outstretched hand. He massaged my fingers for a heartbeat before moving into the required grip. When he was ready, he tugged gently.

This was it. One mistake, and I'd be flat on my back. No crash mats up here. If I landed on the edge of the raised stage holding the pole, I could wind up with a broken back, out of work for months. Any hesitation on my part, and Frank would feel it. I needed to believe in him.

No, I needed to believe in us.

With a deep breath, I let go of the pole with my upper hand. Leaning forward, I grabbed his wrist so I held both his hands. Then I loosened my thighs and contracted my ab muscles, sweeping my feet forward. My legs parted and moved upward as

I swung backwards, supported by nothing but Frank's hand and wrist. In one fluid motion, I turned my body over, coming to rest upside-down, legs parted into a vee shape.

The crowd went wild.

Then Frank looked down at me and mouthed, "I love you."

"I love you, too," I said as the music ended.

He lowered me gently, almost reverently, to the ground before dismounting. We turned to the audience and took our bows. Thunderous applause filled the room. Waves of people shot to their feet, still clapping. A standing ovation! My heart felt so full, I thought it might burst.

Nothing beat the emotional high of knowing that, after everything, we nailed our performance. Frank loved me, I loved him, and everything else would work itself out.

He pulled me into his arms and kissed me again. The applause grew even more thunderous. I threw my arms around him, and the curtain dropped.

THE END

Read on for a sneak peek at *Circle in the Sand* by Tracy Krimmer, the exciting next book in the series!

AUTHOR'S NOTE

First of all, thank you to Delancey Stewart for coming up with the idea for this series and allowing me onboard. Thank you to Holly Kerr and Kirsty McManus for steering the ship, especially when it looked like we were about to hit an iceberg. And thank you to all other authors who embarked on this journey with us: Tracy Krimmer, Holly Tierney-Bedord, Monique McDonell, and Sophie-Leigh Robbins. Learn about the rest of the Oceanic Dream series here:

http://lauraheffernan.com/oceanic-dreams/

I had an enormous amount of fun writing this book. I love cruising, and I got married on a cruise ship. I also did pole fitness for many years before I had to stop due to an injury, and I even helped fill in for the instructor when she wasn't available. This book is dedicated to Heather because she taught me not only how empowering pole could be, but to embrace my inner awesomeness. I will forever be grateful.

Thank you to my fearless critique partners, K.D. Proctor, Marty Mayberry and Kara Reynolds, for your endless patience and insight. I'd be adrift without you.

AMERICA'S NEXT REALITY STAR PREVIEW

America's Next Reality Star

now available from your favorite retailer.

Is it real love or all part of the game?

Life after college isn't as seen on TV: Jen's low-paying job is uninspiring, her boyfriend won't commit, and she just got evicted. The most exercise she gets comes from dodging debt collectors. Then she sees an ad seeking competitors for a new reality show with a $250,000 prize. She desperately needs money and the lottery isn't looking good, so she applies, never expecting to get the call.

Until she does.

With nothing to lose, Jen packs a bag and heads for the Hollywood hills to star in The Fishbowl. Most of the contestants want to create drama to gain viewer votes, but Jen is all about the joy of the game. Unfortunately, she becomes embroiled in a love triangle and battling another woman for the attention of a fellow contestant. It's a tricky balancing act to hold onto viewers without lying, cheating, or backstabbing—things that don't bother her opponents. When Jen discovers that she's on the verge of elimination, she must decide whether "winning" means sacrificing the money, love, or her sense of self.

Read on for a sneak preview!

DO YOU WANT TO WIN $250,000? ARE YOU OUTGOING, VIVACIOUS, AND ENGAGING? DO YOU ALWAYS HAVE TO BE RIGHT? DO YOU LOVE PUZZLES AND TRIVIA? DO YOU USUALLY FIND YOURSELF SURROUNDED BY LESS INTELLIGENT PEOPLE? WE'RE LOOKING FOR SMART, SPUNKY 21 TO 25-YEAR-OLDS, FOR AN EXCITING NEW REALITY COMPETITION FILMING THIS SUMMER! EMAIL STEPHANIE WITH YOUR NAME, AGE, 2-4 PICS, AND A LITTLE ABOUT YOURSELF FOR MORE INFORMATION.

I huddled at my desk, wrapping a blanket over my hoodie. Maybe one day management would trust employees to turn the heat above sixty degrees. Until that glorious day, I held my caffeine molecule-painted mug close to my body, futilely trying to gain warmth from the steam pouring off the top. The coffee tasted like pencil shavings and feet; drinking it wasn't an option.

With my right hand, I scrolled through my Facebook newsfeed, scanning the jokes, cartoons, and mindless banter. It was against the rules, but everyone did it. "Marketing assistant" apparently was code for "exhausting bursts of activity punctuated with lots of sitting around." The irony wasn't lost on me. After working insanely long days all week to include last-minute changes on a major project, I appreciated a few hours' break while my boss reviewed it. The craziness would start again soon enough. I turned up the volume on my computer to project my music over the howling November storm. My toes tapped the linoleum floor.

A message popped up at the bottom of my screen, informing me of a new email. I hit alt-tab to switch programs, expecting the feedback I needed before starting my workday.

No such luck.

It was Seattle General Hospital's billing department. "Dear Ms. Reid, Thank you for your payment..."

Silently, I cursed them for the reminder.

If only the debt could be erased with the same easy click that sent the message to trash. I'd been in perfect health during my high school and college years. So, naturally, my ankle broke a week before my insurance with McCain & Webster kicked in while showing off my impression of Miley Cyrus's latest MTV Music Awards performance. When I slipped on the wet grass and fell, they'd laughed until my tears started. No one realized the fall wasn't part of the act.

Despite my efforts to tough it out ("Unless the bone sticks through the skin, it's fine!"), my boyfriend had dragged me to an Urgent Care facility. Dominic swore it would be affordable. He was half-right: urgent care might have been cheaper than an ER, but the necessary surgery to reset the bone cost a lot. My eyes crossed at the first bill. With my salary, this stupid thing would haunt me until my unborn kids graduated high school. To add insult to (literal) injury, I couldn't figure out how to turn off the automatic emails they sent every month.

I peeked at the empty desk behind me. My officemate would've told me to pretend to work until I got my next assignment. However, he'd left to bond with his newborn daughter. For the next eleven weeks, three days, our tiny office belonged solely to me. I'd been freed from Pete's obnoxious laughter, disapproving looks, and fried fish lunches. With my hall monitor gone and nothing work-related to do for the moment, I checked the bankruptcy qualifications—again—before clicking back to Facebook.

Wait a minute. What was that?

An old college drama professor posted an ad that caught my eye.

A reality show designed for smart people? How intriguing.

Voices buzzed outside my closed door. I glanced nervously over one shoulder. Being located next to the kitchen had its perks, but sometimes I couldn't tell if people were about to burst in on me or just picked an unfortunate spot to gossip.

After deciding my coworkers had gathered to make an early lunch, I read the description again.

Do you want to win $250,000?

It sure beat filing for bankruptcy. There would probably be enough left to go back to school and get a degree in something more interesting. Or maybe put a down payment on a place bigger than a shoebox.

Are you outgoing, vivacious, and engaging?

Well, I liked to think so. All through grade school, I took it upon myself to reach out to new students and make them feel welcome. Now, I hosted parties to celebrate big and small holidays. And I had no problem striking up conversations with random people on the Metro.

Do you always have to be right?

Hmm. I didn't *have* to be right, but I frequently was. I happened to have a good memory. Being able to repeat anything I'd heard came in handy during trivia, mostly. And basement bar debates. Maybe I'd found another use for it.

Do you love puzzles and trivia?

Did owning four themed copies of Trivial Pursuit or spending Metro rides playing Pic-a-Pix and Hashi on my phone count?

Do you usually find yourself surrounded by less intelligent people?

I didn't judge. But I competed on the math and science teams in high school. Some people (those who'd met me) would've said I was kind of a geek. I hoped the show considered that a bonus, since it did nothing for my social life. I didn't go on a single date until my junior year of college.

We're looking for smart, spunky 21 to 25-year-olds.

I was a twenty-one to twenty-five-year-old. Twenty-three, to be exact, turning twenty-four in a few weeks.

As I read through the ad yet again, the little voice in the back of my head piped up. *You should do this*, it said. *Email them.*

What? That was silly. I wasn't an actress—marketing and academics were my bag.

The little voice spoke again. I did love puzzles. I was good at them. The money would be extremely useful. Plus, I couldn't remember my last vacation.

My boyfriend worked as a traveling nurse, which made him less-than-enthusiastic about taking trips with me when he wasn't away on an assignment. I understood. Still, it would be nice to get away, even on my own. What was the time commitment for something like this?

I needed more information.

Before I could chicken out, my fingers opened a new email and began to type as if of their own accord.

Dear Stephanie,

My name is Jennifer Reid, and I'm writing to request more information about your puzzle-based reality show. It sounds like something right up my alley. I'm 23 years old. I live in beautiful Seattle, Washington. It's important to me to live life to the fullest and to grab opportunities when they present themselves.

Since I was a little girl, I've loved puzzles. I chose a career in marketing because I like figuring out what the consumer wants and how to give it to them.

Can you send me more information about the show and when you're looking for someone? Thank you for your time.Best,

Jennifer Reid

Next step, pictures. Which ones to attach? Something showing my face, obviously. But also something fun.

Thanks to the Internet, essentially every picture of me taken over the past six years sat at my fingertips. Thanks to my older brother, Adam, some older and more embarrassing pictures were also there. I bypassed those. The casting director didn't need to see me, at ten, with chocolate cake smeared across my face or four-year-old me waving a cape as I pranced around in Wonder Woman panties, a pink tiara atop blond hair that hadn't yet darkened with age. Thanks, Adam. Twelve-year-old Jen's first attempts at wearing makeup also didn't need to be shared with the world. What had made me think purple eye shadow smeared up to my forehead brought out my blue eyes?

Thanks, Adam, for posting my diving meet pictures where anyone can see them.

It only took a few minutes to find what I wanted. A few years ago, my friends and I went bungee jumping. Someone under the bridge snapped each of us as we took the plunge. My picture showed me falling through the air, head tilted back, arms spread, pure joy on my face.

I had no idea how they caught that expression. I'd been terrified, thought I was going to pee my pants. My breakfast had climbed into my throat, and I'd tamped it down using sheer willpower.

There must be a split second of bliss a person experiences between "Oh, please God, I don't want to die!" and "Why am I doing this?" They happened to click the picture at exactly the right time.

Another great one showed the mess I created trying to cook Dominic dinner for his twenty-fifth birthday (before ordering birthday takeout), but the image focused on the burnt paella, not me. Then I found the perfect shot. While on a trip to New York City, I'd found a sign reading, "This is a library. Quite, please!" My head tilted toward the sign, mouth twisted into a grimace. One hand underlined the word "quite."

I attached it to the email, along with the bungee picture and a regular close-up. Before stopping to consider any potential consequences of my actions, I took a deep breath and hit "send."

A few hours later, my keys jingled as I struggled to unlock my front door. Rainwater dripped from shopping bags balanced on one raised knee. My purse dug into my armpit as I pushed against my apartment door. It stuck. Again. I braced myself against the jamb. One good shove usually did the trick.

My phone, cradled between my chin and shoulder, beeped, startling me. Bags, purse, and umbrella crashed to the floor. An orange rolled out of one bag and down the hall.

Ugh.

As I scrambled to pick everything up, the door swung open. I tensed for a second before my boyfriend's voice sounded from the doorway.

"Oops. So...you got my text?" He crouched beside me and gathered bags.

"Only if it said, 'Hey! Drop everything!'"

As always, seeing Dominic brought a smile to my face. Although we still crouched in the hallway, I leaned over and kissed him.

When we separated, garlic and basil scents wafted by my nose.

Dominic stood and pushed his wavy black hair out of his face with one hand. "Actually, it said, 'When are you going to be home? I have a surprise for you.'"

A grin stretched across my face. He knew how I loved surprises. "You know, you're not supposed to use your key to jump out and scare me."

"What? That's half the fun." His hands now full of my stuff,

Dominic stepped through the door, holding it open as he nodded toward the interior. "After you, gorgeous."

As soon as I entered my four-hundred-square-foot apartment, I spotted the surprise. Freshly baked garlic bread steamed on the two-person wooden table, next to a tossed Caesar salad and spaghetti with homemade meatballs. My mouth watered.

I popped onto my toes and planted a kiss on his cheek. "You are the best boyfriend ever."

"I know. I'm having a T-shirt made."

Dominic's lips hovered over mine. My arms wrapped around his neck, and I rose up to meet him before allowing myself to sink into the kiss. After a moment, he picked me up and spun me onto the kitchen counter. My legs wrapped around his waist as his hands cupped my face.

God, I loved him.

We'd met my last year in college, when he was a graduate student. I'd been attracted to his rugged good looks and liked that he wasn't clingy or demanding. We had fun together, but he didn't complain when I worked overtime or spent time with my girlfriends. A year later, I'd already caught myself looking at engagement rings.

Er...just the one time, though. We had plenty of time for that later.

Dominic's hand found the clasp to my bra—we hadn't seen each other in more than a week. However, my body interrupted the kiss by emitting a sound that was less a growl of hunger and more the howl of a wild animal being murdered. Dominic pulled back, gave me one last kiss, then set me onto the floor.

I gazed at the tiles, hoping he didn't see the mortification on my face. "Sorry. I took an early lunch."

"Don't be sorry." With a sweeping bow, he indicated the table. "Your feast awaits."

A piece of garlic bread disappeared into my mouth as I sat, surveying the table. "This looks amazing! Thank you!"

"You're welcome." A slow, lazy smile spread across his face. My stomach flip-flopped. "You've been working so hard, I figured you probably weren't eating right."

I speared a meatball with my fork. "You're a smart man. It's been mostly canned tuna or Lunchables in my office at ten p.m."

Dominic shuddered. "Lunchables?"

"Eight days in a row. Luckily, I get a few days' reprieve before it picks up again."

"Ew. You poor thing. Well, I brought a ton of food and Tupperware, so you're set for at least a week."

Reaching across the table, I took his hand in mine and squeezed. My skin tingled at the contact. "Thank you. That helps a lot."

We didn't talk about it, but Dominic knew I couldn't afford to eat well. The fact that he'd gone out of his way to make me lunch for several days sent butterflies fluttering in my belly.

"You're welcome, babe. Next time things get crazy, promise you'll call me so I can bring you a real meal? Or have one delivered so I don't interrupt you?"

Cheesy-noodle-and-marinara-saucy-goodness glued my mouth shut, so I nodded. His twinkling brown eyes captured mine. A spark of lust sent my thoughts away from dinner and onto a more interesting path. Dominic's dilating pupils told me his thoughts followed the same route. I chewed faster as a familiar thrill of anticipation spread through my body.

Dominic's hand wrapped around mine. I pushed the plate away and stood. Our lips met. We didn't quite make it to the bedroom.

The reminder that I had a good thing with Dominic in Seattle pushed my reality show application out of my mind. There were other ways to make extra cash. I arrived at work the next morning dreaming about the next step in our relationship. We'd been dating for over a year, and he'd had a key to my apartment for months. I'd have his, too, as soon as I figured out where it had disappeared to, hours after he'd given it to me.

Lost in thought, I walked to my desk and opened my email. A new message appeared from someone named Stephanie Long. Who? I didn't know anyone named Stephanie.

Subject: Re: Casting call.

Oh. My. God.

My heart beat faster.

Dear Jennifer,

Thank you so much for your interest in our new series. *The Fishbowl* is a fast-paced reality show with physical and mental challenges to push the contestants on every level. What makes this different from other shows is that viewers vote on aspects of the game. With things always changing, you'll never know what to expect!

Filming will start at the beginning of June. We estimate that contestants could be on the show as few as a couple of days or as long as ten weeks.

Our team is interviewing applicants across the country now. We'll be in Seattle next week and would love to meet you. Please call my assistant at 323-555-1258 to set up an interview.

Best,

Stephanie

The viewers would tell us what to do? On live television? Huh. What if they made us eat bugs? I'd have to ask the interviewer. But otherwise—up to three months in LA? New people and new experiences? It sounded interesting, but I wasn't sure I could afford to take that much time away from work. Or my boyfriend.

On the other hand, it would be fun to surprise Dominic if I made the show. And our relationship had never been stronger.

We could handle time apart. Between my overtime and his traveling to care for patients, we didn't exactly hang out every day.

Hey, honey, your girlfriend's going to win loads of money on a reality show so we can buy a house...

I reached to call Stephanie's assistant practically before I finished reading.

☾

On Wednesday morning, I showed up at the address they'd given me. Peeling paint, boarded-up windows, and several "Space for Rent" signs against a backdrop of drizzle and gray morning light welcomed me. Trash spilled out of the can next to the front door. A rat scurried away down an alley. It seemed odd to think my fate might lie within this dilapidated building.

Sure, Jen, lots of women's fates lie in old, run-down buildings. But is that the way you want to go?

I double-checked the address on my phone. Google informed me I stood in the right spot. As I hesitated, remembering that guy who picked up women on Craigslist and murdered them, the front door opened. A girl about my age walked out wearing red tights and a blue shirt that didn't look as much like a dress as she must've thought. Sunglasses covered the top half of her face, so I couldn't tell if she noticed me as she tottered past on five-inch turquoise heels, chatting on her phone.

"Yeah, I just left the interview. It's totally not a beauty contest..."

Was that what I should've worn to the interview?

My black pants and red button-up shirt with matching red and black polka-dotted ballet flats were appropriate for going to work when I finished, but now they made me look boring. My own heels lived in a drawer in my desk, to be taken out upon my arrival at the office. Were the producers looking for people who dressed more colorfully?

Only one way to find out.

Taking a deep breath, I smoothed my hair and entered. A layer of dust on the empty sign-in desk suggested no one had welcomed visitors to this building since the Reagan administration. A curved staircase stretched ahead of me. A hand-lettered sign next to the mailboxes informed me that ABC Casting could be found on the second floor. It didn't seem worth looking for an elevator.

My foot caught almost immediately on a missing step. Awesome. I clutched at the decrepit-looking metal railing. It wobbled, but thankfully held.

I hadn't been cast yet, and already someone was trying to kill me. Were there cameras in the stairwell?

I righted myself and let go before the railing snapped beneath the unexpected weight. Then I peeked behind me. Nothing else dangerous lurked in the dim light. The dark corners of the ceiling probably didn't hide cameras.

It was probably an old building, not a trap. Sometimes, I had an overactive imagination. Still, I proceeded carefully to the stop of the stairs. Thankfully, no other missing steps or holes in the floor jumped into my path.

The producers must have just set up the room for these interviews. Nothing hung on the white walls. Someone had shoved a lumpy beige couch against one wall with a couple of armchairs overturned on top of it. End tables piled in front of the couch dissuaded anyone who might have considered clearing it. A card table stood in the middle of the room, buried under stacks of paper. Extension cords snaked around the industrial beige carpet.

A guy in his late twenties, medium build and height, with floppy brown hair and a wrinkled shirt greeted me with a grin.

His unkempt appearance made me feel better about not dressing like a fashion model.

He looks so normal. Definitely a serial killer. Like John Wayne Gacy.

"Hey! I'm John," he said, shaking my hand before settling into a folding chair behind the table.

Wayne Gacy? I asked myself before I could help it. Then I shoved those thoughts aside. That line of thinking wouldn't lead to a productive interaction.

"I'm Jen. It's nice to meet you." I moved a laptop off the only other chair. Unsure what to do, I offered it to him.

"Sorry. Thanks. We're casting for a brand-new show here, like nothing you've seen. There will be puzzles, physical challenges, and more. Contestants will push themselves on all levels. It's not a beauty contest, and it's not for the faint of heart."

I nodded. I'd learned all that from the ad and Stephanie's email. "That's exactly what I'm looking for."

"Excellent! So, why do you want to be on television?"

"My personal hero is Eleanor Roosevelt. She said that life is for living, for grabbing onto each new experience and savoring it. I believe that. So, for me, it's more about wanting to experience new things and explore every opportunity. This seems like a great way to meet new people, and I love puzzles, trivia, and games. Plus, I'm broke. I could really use $250,000. So when I read the ad, it was like it was shouting, 'Jen, come be on our show.' It's exactly what I need right now."

He consulted his clipboard. "You said you like games. What was your favorite toy as a child?"

Some people might have had to think before answering this question, but I'd done a lot of research and prepared my answers. "My older brother's Erector Set. I used to sneak into his room to build pyramids when he played baseball." I laughed. "He never figured out why pieces sometimes went missing."

John smiled. "Sounds like he should have let you play with him. Did you go to college?"

"Yup! University of Washington, Class of 2012! Go Huskies!"

"Okay," John said. "Tell me this. If you were out in Seattle at a bar with your friends and a guy sat down to talk to you, what is the one thing he would be absolutely shocked to find out about you?"

Without missing a beat, I offered a big, sweet smile. "I'm an assassin."

John showed me the whites of his eyes. Then he pushed his chair back from the table and shivered in exaggerated fear.

We both laughed. "Okay, I'm not. I'm pretty normal." I let my mind roam for a moment. "You may not believe this because I'm fairly small, but a few years ago I won a hot dog eating contest."

"What? No way!" He gasped in mock disbelief.

"Absolutely!" I flexed my biceps, preening for a moment. "Of course, the only other person who entered was seventy years old; he ate three. Grandpa might have let me win."

"A win's a win, right?" He consulted his papers. "Okay, that's everything I needed to ask you. Do you have any questions for me? Questions about the show, the process? My favorite color?"

"I did wonder about one thing. The email said the viewers would tell us what to do?"

"Right. They'll vote on things like which mini-challenge to do, which player deserves to be up for elimination, and things like that."

"Okay, so they're not voting to make us do bizarre or disgusting things?"

"Like what?"

"Like...eating bugs? Cleaning the toilet with our tooth-brushes?"

He laughed. "No, no. Nothing like that. This isn't Fear Factor."

My shoulders sagged with relief. "Awesome. Then it's all good. I'm excited."

"Great! We're excited, too! I need a four to six minute video by the end of the week, telling me who you are, what you do, your hobbies—basically, why we should pick you. If you Google it, you can find audition videos from other shows to get an idea of what we're looking for. Anything else?"

I consulted the list on my phone, although I'd memorized it three days ago. "Can you tell me about the casting process?"

"People who make it to the next round will fly to Los Angeles for a screen test, IQ tests, a medical exam, psych tests, etc. Then we'll do background checks on the people we choose. The finalists will be notified a couple of weeks later. It's pretty straightforward. The hardest part is waiting."

"Makes sense. Thanks."

John stood and shook my hand. "Great. Thanks for coming in, Jennifer. We'll be in touch."

I thanked him, and that was it. The whole thing took less than half an hour.

After carefully navigating the stairs, I left the interview with a smile on my face and a spring in my step. Since I'd taken the entire morning off work, I decided to walk to the office. Most likely, I'd need to stay late; a new project could hit my desk any minute.

Regardless of the dark and gloomy skies, a beautiful day peeked from behind the backdrop of the old buildings. My feet danced around the puddles, oblivious to the rain streaming around me. When the wind fought to steal my umbrella, it didn't faze me.

Rather than rush back to the grind, I stopped at a coffee shop to read the application John gave me. I'd told my boss I had an appointment and didn't know how long it would take. When I implied I needed personal time, he'd assumed that meant a gynecologist appointment. He wrung his hands and prohibited me from sharing any details before rushing me out of his office. Men.

Reading the application made me laugh at how thorough the producers were. They asked about everything.

What kind of people did I dislike?

Mean people, bigots, and people who text during movies on giant phones that light up the theater.

What would I do with an extra five grand?

Owe five grand less to Seattle General? Or buy a new purse and owe $4,980 less.

How do other people see me?

With their eyeballs, usually.

What would I do if I knew no one would ever catch me?

Break into Fort Knox. Or maybe Buckingham Palace.

How would I describe myself in twenty-five words or fewer?

I'm a twenty-three-year-old marketing assistant, completely unchallenged. I make no money and live in the world's smallest apartment. Being an adult sucks.

Hmm...maybe I should go back to that one later. I kept reading. What clubs or organizations did I belong to? If I could have plastic surgery on any part of my body, which one and why?

Any part? Like, could I walk around with giant earlobes or add fingers to my elbows? That would be a conversation starter.

What was my height/weight? My dress/ring/shoe/hat size? Hat size? I had no idea. I had to measure my head. How cool was that?

It was like completing the world's most interesting job application. Still, after the ninth or tenth page, I expected them to ask my favorite brand of dental floss or whether I preferred one- or two-ply toilet paper (For the record: Oral B, and two.) My favorite part was the self-portrait.

Luckily, the coffee shop provided crayons for children and,

apparently, reality-show hopefuls. Since my eyes were my best feature, I started with the blue crayon. Some quick brown strokes filled in my hair. How realistic did this have to be? I mean, I could give myself a button nose right? Maybe soften my chin?

After a few minutes, I leaned back and scrutinized my work. Hmm. I may have gone overboard. Or maybe Cartoon Jen wears Wonderbras. I added an asterisk.

Note: Not to scale.

For good measure, I sketched a party hat on my head and some board games in the background. A red crayon added a smile I hoped looked friendly, not manic. Perfect.

I hoped that, next time I applied for a job or promotion, they requested a self-portrait enclosed with my résumé. Maybe I'd add one. I pictured the cover letter: "I have attached a résumé for your consideration, along with a self-portrait of how happy I'd be in this position."

When I reached my office, I was still laughing at the silliness of the whole process.

MORE BY LAURA HEFFERNAN

The Reality Star Series

America's Next Reality Star: Jen went on a reality show to compete for the $250,000 grand prize. But when she finds herself battling another woman for co-competitor Justin's love, she finds herself wondering what the true prize is.

Sweet Reality: After a killer competitor threatens her new business, Jen sets sail on a new reality show adventure to save the day. But Ariana's back, and she's determined to end Jen and Justin's relationship once and for all.

Reality Wedding: After retiring from reality TV, Jen receives an offer she can't refuse. The Network wants Jen and Justin to film their wedding to fill an empty time slot—and if they refuse, the Network will get Justin fired.

The Gamer Girls Series

She's Got Game: Gwen's dedicated to becoming the American Board Games Champion, and she never ever mixes gaming with pleasure. But when she meets Cody, trying to resist his charm becomes a losing proposition.

Against the Rules: For years, Holly has harbored a secret crush on her best friend's dad. Nathan is young, he's hot. What's a little harmless flirtation while playing games? But when she discovers that Nathan returns her feelings, Holly may have to choose between two of the most important people in her life.

❧

Push and Pole Series

Poll Dancer: A delightfully modern twist on *My Fair Lady*: When a promotional video for her pole-dancing classes goes viral, Mel comes under fire from a local politician running for senate. Desperate to save her studio, Mel decides her only option is to launch her own campaign — and win!

The Accidental Senator: After accidentally finding herself elected state senator, Lana Chen is determined to prove her worth. But when a mistake aids the passage of a bill that's going to put her best friend out of business, Lana has to find a way to set things right before it's too late.

❧

Retail to Riches Series

A Royal Farce: After years of secretly crushing on her friend Pierre, Lila is thrilled when he proposes they start a fake relationship. For weeks, she finds herself hoping their farce could turn into the real thing—but Pierre's hiding a secret of royal magnitude.

A Royal Pain: **Coming Soon**

❧

Standalone Books

Finding Tranquility: Jess Cooper lost her husband on 9/11. Just not the way she thought. On September 11, 2001, Brett enters Logan Airport bearing a ticket for a flight that crashes into the World Trade Center. Jess knows her husband is gone. She doesn't know he never boarded that plane. Years later, Jess is shocked to meet Christa and recognize her spouse. She's more shocked to realize their love may have survived.

Anna's Guide to Getting Even: Anna's perfect life has turned into a string of disasters: After a hurricane destroys her house, her ex publicizes private photos of her — which costs Anna her job and her current boyfriend. And after hitting rock bottom, she decides that revenge is the only way forward...

Friction: Britt's always avoided relationships. Then, weeks before she's set to move away, she meets Colin. To her surprise, she finds herself wanting more.

Time of My Life: She's a poor dance teacher. He's her rich student. If they can only overcome their differences, this could be love. A gender-flipped update of *Dirty Dancing.*

ABOUT THE AUTHOR

Laura Heffernan is like the wind. A couple of years ago, she discovered that she could have the time of her life doing pole fitness. In the still of the night, Laura enjoys writing books that recognize love is strange.

Before taking time off to have a baby, yes, she could do most of the moves described in this book. Not that one. But because big girls don't cry, she tries not to dwell on it. Where are you tonight? Probably on Twitter, tweeting about reality television, board games, or Canadian chocolate.

Read about Laura's other books at www.lauraheffernan.com or sign up for her newsletter at http://eepurl.com/clbuoP.

Future scientists don't have visions. Aly's got enough on her plate, with finishing her degree and taking care of her nephew and starting her new job at the antique store while drooling over the owner's gorgeous son. No visions.

Alas, the universe doesn't care what Aly believes. When she turns 21, she starts to feel psychic impressions left on objects. A disorienting power for someone surrounded by antiques. Then cranky customer Earl is killed, and Aly's new boss Olive is the prime suspect. Who hated Earl enough to kill? Police would rather make a quick arrest than investigate, so it's up to Aly to clear Olive's name.

Shady Grove is reeling from the first murder in decades. If Aly can get her hands on the murder weapon, she should be able to solve the crime. Can she learn to control her visions before the killer sets their sights on her?

Mystic Pieces
The Scry's the Limit
Sight Seering
Mystic Treasure
Seer Today, Gone Tomorrow